# The Temptress Ariel

By
Greg Bauder

PublishAmerica
Baltimore

© 2004 by Greg Bauder.
All rights reserved. No part of this book may be reproduced, stored in a retrieval system or transmitted in any form or by any means without the prior written permission of the publishers, except by a reviewer who may quote brief passages in a review to be printed in a newspaper, magazine or journal.

First printing

ISBN: 1-4137-3296-8
PUBLISHED BY PUBLISHAMERICA, LLLP
www.publishamerica.com
Baltimore

Printed in the United States of America

⚡ **For My Dad** ⚡

## Chapter 1

I STUMBLED INTO LOVE WITH THE NEW WOMAN, ARIEL, WHO MOVED INTO THE Psychiatric Boarding Home. She was small and slightly chubby, proud as a pampered cat, and she had big, owl eyes. But her smile intrigued me most: it came easy, and I knew there would be competition to kiss it. My pale hands shook with desire as I began my plans to see if she was interested in me; she seemed solid and bright, unlike most of the burnt-out, ghostly people here. I was so paranoid that Murray would want her; he was as solid as me and never Jonsed out. I started feeling light and I rolled over on my back on my bed; my hard-on always made my body a little emptier.

Was I dreaming? No, I heard her in the hallway talking to Murray! Holy shit! I ran out of my room into the shaggy-carpeted hall. There was only a thin man pacing, pausing to stretch his back every two or three steps. I didn't question him because he'd just tell me to stop bothering him. I entered the living-room and I saw her. She was more beautiful than any woman I could imagine. So she was real. I sat next to her. Her perfume was intoxicating and I hoped it wouldn't put Murray on her trail.

"Hi," I said. "My name's Don."

"I'm Ariel," she smiled seductively. "Are you going for meds?" I was high, as her dark eyelashes fluttered. I was in over my head but I was happier than an angel.

"Yeah."

"What are you on?"

"Haldol, Luvox, and Clonazepam," I replied. "How about yourself?"

"Nothing," she said, and she opened a paper white hand with pills. She winked. "See you later and please, mum's the word." She rose. I watched her smile that smile over her shoulder as she entered her room down the hall. Slightly dazed, I rise and get my meds. The nurse said I seemed chipper today. I took it to mean I had a chip on my shoulder with Murray. The staff always watch like eagles, ready to lift you away to hospital if you feel too light. I mumbled a thank-you and took my pills. But I was wary of my rival.

I went back to my room. My thoughts were racing as fast as ants on an ant hill. Maybe I was being foolish. Her name... Ariel...she could be something wild on the hunt for game . Maybe a mind game. I sat on my bed with possibilities dancing favorably with her. My arms around her, kissing those Sheryl Crow lips. It mad me happy, and I grinned to myself. But how could I love a woman I'd only just met? I wavered with suspicion. Then I am loving her again, touching her bleach-white breasts and licking her pacifying nipples. I rested until I heard the call for dinner.

The next chance I got to talk to her came after dinner. I was sitting in the living room on a couch watching Much Music (which was on about half of every day here it seemed) when she sat down beside me as though it were the last empty seat on a bus.

"Your name's Don, right?" She smiled. Oh, that enticing smile.

"Yeah, and you're Ariel, right?" She nodded, and then I asked her what she thought of dinner.

"I liked it, especially the sausages. And the peas and carrots."

"It was nice and hot, too," I replied. "Arlene can sure cook up a storm."

"Yeah, I agree. So... Don, how long have you been living here?"

"About five years."

"Do you work or go to school?"

"I work part time. At the food bank. I'm a volunteer."

"I see," she said. "Come into the smoking room and have a smoke with me, okay? We'll talk some more."

"I don't smoke, but I'll join you anyhow."

"Maybe we can change you of that non-habit" She smiled, flicking her eyelashes. "Let's go."

We both rose and entered the smoking-room.

There was only one light person in there smoking. His name was Chet and he was very ill. He looked at Ariel and me.

"Chet, have you met Ariel?" I asked, as Ariel sat on a chair like a cat on its haunches. She reached into her jean jacket pocket and pulled out a cigarette. She was so gorgeous that I yearned to kiss her siren lips.

"Yes, I have," said Chet, who wore thick-lensed glasses. "But, I don't know if she believes in God."

"I do in my own way," she said.

"Same here," I added. I was pleased with her response because I had met many religious fanatics who were mentally ill and would Jones out if they talked about demons and Satan.

"So .... how come you're here, Don ? What happened to you?" She inquired with that smile. I wanted to kiss her all over. Like that old song that popped into my head just then.

"I broke down after my Mom died and my girlfriend left me. I started to hear demons and see space-ships at night. They drove me crazy. I was left totally alone on the streets and I finally ended up in the Psych Ward. I was always shy and withdrawn; a timid turtle, you might say." I was proud of that simile. "How about you, Ariel?"

"Oh, I tried to kill myself when my horse Stan.... I mean ....Teddy died. I love to ride in the country. But I was in hospital for a bit and now I'm here. But, someday I'll get another horse." She puffed on her cigarette staring sadly straight ahead, but I knew she was conscious of me watching her. Then, Chet finished his cigarette and left. I felt a little more solid gazing at her all to myself.

"I hope you get another horse soon," I said sympathetically. I was relieved when her smile returned. I loved her more because she was a caring person. I believed she had a Midas heart.

"So, what do you people do around here for excitement?" she said suddenly eager, her eyes shining.

"Not much," I said, startled. "Watch TV, listen to music, read, go on outings."

"Do you ever go to the Pub?" she asked almost mischieviously.

"Well....no....we're not allowed," I answered uncertainly. "Most of us are on medication. Plus, hardly any of us can afford to go." I hoped she caught my meaning.

"Well, you must have money because you don't smoke and all your living expenses are paid for here. Plus you work a little and that probably helps you save a bit of money."

"Yeah, you're right, I have saved a little....I guess we could go if you want to," I said a little shakily, but she didn't seem to notice, which hurt me a tiny bit. I wanted to please her desperately, even though I barely knew her.

"Well, grab your jacket and let's go!" she exclaimed, as she put out her cigarette butt.

"Okay," I replied. I didn't really want to go, but I felt I might come across to her as selfish if I didn't go. So, I got my coat, and we told the nurses we were going for coffee. We signed out on the blackboard, and ran through the doors like a pair of wild horses. I could hear a nurse behind us telling us to slow down. There was a trace of mistrust in her voice. Ariel and I stopped running once we'd crossed the yard and met the sidewalk.

"O'Reilly's is just down the street about a block," Ariel said.

"I know. I've been by it many times."

"And you've never gone in?" she asked, incredulously.

"No."

"Well, we'll have to have a few. It'll be a nice change from that dull boarding-home."

We walked in silence the rest of the way to the Pub and I began to sense Ariel's excitement rising with mine. I opened the door to the Pub, and Ariel and then I walked in. It was dimly lit and the atmosphere was warm and hummed with conversations. We sat down in a booth and took our jackets off, looking at each other, scarcely noticing the sparse crowd in there. Then, a waitress appeared and asked us what we'd like.

"I'll have a white rum and coke. A double. Neat," Ariel said to her.

"I'll have the same," I said nervously.

The waitress smiled and left with our orders. I leaned over the table to get closer to Ariel and asked her in a low tone how much the drinks would cost.

"About six bucks each," she said.

"I've only got twenty dollars on me. Do they have an instabank here?"

"Yeah , follow me," she answered.

We rose and went to the machine. I felt Ariel's arm through mine as I punched in my personal code and took out sixty dollars. Ariel kissed me on the cheek, and whispered in my ear that the good times were just beginning, as we returned to the booth. The waitress arrived with our drinks just as we settled into the booth, so I paid for them with a twenty. I told the waitress to keep a dollar for herself. She thanked me as I looked at Ariel, who then took a big gulp of the rum and coke. I hoped she was not an alcoholic. Whatever, I still loved her; everybody has their hangups— or in this case maybe hangovers— and I began to grin as I also took a big draught of my drink which tasted warm and wonderful. It had been a long time since I'd gone drinking alcohol. I hoped we wouldn't get too light and Jones out, I think I said aloud. But Ariel was busy taking another big gulp. I was feeling like we were at a 7-11 store the way we were drinking.

"So, Don, tell me, have you been involved with any women recently?" Ariel asked me as we
drank slightly slower.

"Not for quite a few years," I responded. I looked deep into her leather brown eyes.

"How many's quite a few?"

"A few too many. Maybe six, seven years."

"I think we could be close friends," she said. "Don't you think so?" she added coyly.

"I hope so," I said, as I felt the warmth from her voice and the rum.

The waitress came around just as we finished our drinks, so Ariel and I ordered the same drinks. We sat in silence for a minute, looking about and revelling in the Pub. The waitress arrived with our drinks. I paid her, and again I was enchanted by Ariel's beauty and mannerisms. Even the way she held her cigarette high turned me on. But I was worried about her not taking her meds.

"How come you don't take your meds?" I blurted out, surprising myself and her. "I know it's up to you, but do you think you're doing the right thing?"

"I don't believe in medication ," she said, staring down at her drink. She gulped the rest of it down. I followed her by guzzling my drink down. "I only take medications in hospitals," she continued. "Once I'm out, I palm them. I've gotten good at it."

"Are you sure you know what you're doing?" I continued rather doggedly, noticing that I had slurred my "s" on "sure." The waitress came around with more drinks that I didn't remember ordering. I paid her as my blood surged, impassioned by Ariel. I was feeling light but not a psychotic light.

"Yeah, I know what I'm doing. The question is, do you?" Ariel asked with a giggle.

"I'm serious," I said. She seemed a little angry, as her eyes narrowed like a cat's when forced from a comfortable lap. Suddenly, she began crying. I placed my hand on hers, her small fingers warming my heart.

"What's wrong, Ariel? I hope I didn't upset you– I'm just concerned, that's all," I remarked, frightened.

"It's not you, Don. I like you. But, remember when I said I broke down over my horse dying? Well, that's only partly true," she said, looking at her glass, "because when I was young I was– I was – molested."

I gave her my napkin, and she wiped her tears. We both took a sip of our drinks in silence. I wanted to console her with the right words, make her happy.

"You're the most beautiful and interesting woman I've ever met!" I blurted out, aware that I was trying to help her, and at the same time expressing my infatuation with her without being too glib or corny, I hoped. Her eyelashes fluttered like wings.

"Thank you, Don," she said, a smile rekindling her face. I was feeling good, but I didn't know how much affect she was having on me because of the rum. But I loved the excitement that came from being with her, being seen with her, as the bar bubbled with intense chatter. I looked around and then glanced at my watch. I was so happy to be with Ariel and her pill-round face. I began to laugh and she cornered me with a question. I said I was laughing at an old joke, not at her. She gave me a strange look.

"I'm glad we came here, Ariel," I said.

"How about if we finish these drinks and go?" Ariel asked. I felt somewhat guilty for looking at my watch, but I was grateful for her discernment, so I smiled at her. "Otherwise the staff might wonder why we were away so long."

I loved how she seemed to accept me, warped and all. I looked at my watch again. A time warp.

"Yesh," I slured, and we both laughed.

She tossed her long black hair, and then smoothed it back with her dove-white hands in a way that was arousing. We finished our drinks and edged our way to the door through the now crowded bar. As we left the pub, the cool October evening met us with a pressing wind. And I wanted to press Ariel to me, hang on to her forever. We walked down the steps and I felt surprise and elation when her lamb-soft hand was somehow in my hand. I was not sure if it was my move or hers, but I looked deep into the pools of her eyes and suddenly our lips and tongues were like blissful, slippery seals. We didn't care that cars were passing by as we embraced– a moment that extinguished our surroundings.

All too soon we unlocked and began walking the street towards the boarding home. A lock-up of a different kind.

I was even more aroused as we walked the streets in silence since we kept glancing at each other and smiling. How can a woman's smile be so sexy? Suddenly, Ariel stopped walking and began to cry. I held her close, stroking her soft, feathery hair, asking her what was wrong. Fear closes in on me when someone is starting to Jones, but I began speaking to her soothingly, telling her to let her depression out.

"He was a preacher. A hypocrite preacher who used to touch me and my friends. He told us not to tell.....Don....I hope you still like me." Ariel's eyes were jelly with tears as she looked at me with pain contorting her face. I was helpless, wanting to erase the past scars that were tormenting her.

"Of course I like you, Ariel."

"Kiss me," she said, and we began making lip service to each other but not without me recognizing, even drunk, that her yo-yo moods meant that she probably had bi-polar disorder. I had met other mentally ill people with this mood swing affliction, and usually they took Lithium and other medications for it. I was feeling sick, suddenly, unable to tell her again that she needed to take her pills.

We reached the boarding home without holding hands so that the nurses wouldn't watch our every move. We told the staff that we had two drinks each. The evening nurse reminded us that alcohol and our medications do not mix well. She warned us to stay away from the pubs.

I went to my room after thanking Ariel for the outing. I lay on my bed after taking my coat off. The bed seemed to spin like a carnival ride. But my thoughts were spinning more about Ariel. I was in love. I had only loved one girl before: Sylvia, my ex-fiancee who had committed suicide when I was in my third year of college. My mind was racing like a greyhound as I rested on my bed. Finally, the nine o'clock call for meds came through on the intercom. But I didn't move. My memories of Sylvia attacked my mind– how I had found out that she had cheated on me with a friend of mine. I was hurt and adamantly stood back from reconciliation. It was just after we broke up that my mother died of cancer. I guessed that since Sylvia and my mother had been very close, and I was unforgiving, she couldn't carry on.

I rolled over and sat on the edge of my bed. For the first time I realized that maybe Sylvia's death wasn't about me. I remembered how her grades had slipped after her affair with my friend. And how she'd had an abusive childhood like Ariel's. I was beginning to notice that Ariel was allowing me to see that forgiving was better than forgetting. I no longer wanted to suppress my emotions and remain bitter. Ariel was re-opening my heart. I began to cry away my tears of pent-up anguish over Sylvia.

The intercom buzzed again, and I responded by wiping my tears and leaving my room. Murray passed me by in the hall and asked me if I was Jonesing a bit. I told him I was okay as I entered the door of the nurses' office. Sarah the nurse looked at me, sizing up my emotional state.

"Would you like to talk?" she asked, handing me my meds. I hesitated, then said yes. Before long, I had spewed out my feelings about Sylvia and how I was afraid of becoming close to Ariel.

"Don't forget that you've been drinking tonight. And don't expect Ariel to be the answer to your problems. Relationships are hard work. Many mentally ill people are incapable of forming a loving relationship because of their inability to trust and cope. But you are fairly well and have a better chance than most. Just be careful, go slow, and— above all— communicate. Okay?" she asked, smiling.

"Yeah," I said, and we rose and hugged. Just then, Ariel came into the office doorway.

"Can I have my pills when you two are through?" she asked, angry as a disturbed honeybee.

"We were just talking about the painful feelings I'm dealing with since I met you. My– "

"Oh, so I'm hard to deal with, Don!" Ariel cried, tears squirting down her cheeks.

"Let him finish, Ariel," the nurse said gently.

"Ariel," I said, "I was talking to Sarah about my ex-girlfriend who committed suicide. Her name was Sylvia. I haven't been close to a woman since her. I have rarely even thought of her, until I met you. You've stirred up a lot of feelings in me. Sarah was just helping me with my fears. Honest." My voice began to shake. "I want us to be close, Ariel."

"I'm sorry, Don," Ariel said. "I know you care. Besides, now that I think of it, if you two had something going on, you wouldn't hug with the office door open where other staff and residents could see you."

"Thanks, Ariel," I said, with a big sigh of relief, as the nurse popped Ariel's pills out of the bubble package on the white medication desk.

Ariel put the pills in her mouth and drank the orange juice in the blue med cup. I followed her out of the office, hoping she hadn't "cheeked" her pills. She glanced over her shoulder with that winning smile at me; then, she entered the women's washroom. When I heard the toilet flush I was concerned and frightened for Ariel. I knew when the medication was out of her system, she would be on the way to a psychotic episode. I hoped she would change her mind. But, in the meantime, I would refuse to rat on her.

I went back to my room feeling down. My CD/Cassette player on top of my brown dresser suddenly called me into the refuge and therapy of music. I put on my favourite tape: The Who's *Who's Next*. I somehow managed to forget my problems, until halfway through the tape I heard a tapping at my door. I opened the door to see Ariel's gorgeous face, her eyes bright as candles. She was wearing a pink terry-cloth robe as well as soft pink slippers.

"I just wanted to say goodnight, Don," she said in an uncharacteristic, bashful tone. I smiled at her." I know it's a little early to be going to bed, but I just wanted to see you. I hope you don't mind," she added, while her eyes were taking in my modest furnishings: single bed, night-table with a radio alarm clock on it, two dressers (one with a mirror and the other with my CD/Casstte player) and boxes of dusty books on the floor and in my open closet.

"It's still a little early for me to go to bed," I responded, looking at my watch. So I'm going to play The Who for awhile. But I'll be thinking of you and I hope you have a good night's sleep. Hopefully we can be together tomorrow."

"I'm sure we can," she smiled, like a sunny day, I thought. Then I gave her a quick kiss on her sensual mouth.

We both said goodnight and I watched her sexy saunter down the hallway. I closed my door, my mind mulling over this sweet little temptress. I couldn't concentrate on The Who's music for the first time in years, my thoughts were so filled with Ariel. So, I went to bed early and scarcely slept that night. I was afraid of her and for her. I resolved to talk to her again about taking her meds.

## Chapter 2

I AWOKE WITH A HEADACHE, AND REALIZED IMMEDIATELY THAT I HAD A hangover from the rum. I hoped Ariel felt okay, as I remembered our time together yesterday. My window was golden with sunshine as I dressed and groomed myself. I hadn't felt such happiness and excitement for many years. Yet, I was anxious and feeling a little light and almost liquidy.

I looked at my radio alarm clock just then, and I noticed I had gotten up a half hour early. The nurse hadn't even buzzed my room for meds. So, I went to get my meds, and maybe have some toast for breakfast. As I arrived at the nurses' office — with no sign of Ariel around, much to my disappointment — the head nurse informed me that there was to be no more intoxication in the boarding home. She said it was dangerous to mix our medications with alcohol, especially for Ariel who was on higher doses of medication than I was. I apologized, and told her I would try to avoid drinking in the future.

After I swallowed my meds, I went into the kitchen and was joyfully surprised to see Ariel making toast. She was wearing tight jeans, with knee-high black boots and a heavy white sweater. Her hair was done up at the back so that it didn't flow the way I liked it, but to me she was the most beautiful woman I had ever seen. I was thrilled when she smiled, said good morning, and asked me if I'd like some toast and strawberry jam. I wanted to hug her and kiss her but held back like a bridled horse.

"I'd love some toast," I said, "but maybe with a little honey. Not from you, from the jar in the cupboard."

"You're so sweet to say that," she beamed, and it was then that I knew I was in love with her. I had rarely handed out such compliments to women with such ease, and my heart was beating fast.

The four pieces of toast popped up just then, and I stood very close to her and asked her if I could help. She smiled and told me to sit in the dining-room; she would bring in breakfast for me. I sat in one of the brown wooden chairs facing the cheerful, flowery wallpaper with its red and yellow roses. I felt a little like Pavlov's dog, only I wasn't salivating for breakfast, I wanted to taste Ariel's kisses.

My mind was so preoccupied that I had failed to notice my friend Murray sitting on the other side of the room. He waved and asked me how I was doing. I said I was doing fine and he replied likewise. Then, Ariel brought in the toast and orange juice, placing my plate on the white placemat in front of me. But I was surprised when she turned around and put the other plate before Murray. I was doing my best to control my anger, as I asked Ariel why she wasn't eating with me.

"Oh, I never eat breakfast," she smiled. "But, I do like to cook, especially for you."

"And Murray," I said almost bitterly, feeling less solid.

"Oh, Don, no!" she exclaimed, her eyes shocked like an eagle's stare. "I made Murray breakfast because he gave me two cigarettes. I was all out." Tears started to roll down her face as she turned and left the dining room, her boots stomping like drum-beats on the linoleum floor. I rose and followed her but she ducked into her room before I could catch up to her.

I knocked on her door, asking her if we could talk.

"Not, now Don. I'm very upset."

"I'm sorry, Ariel. I guess I was being paranoid," I pleaded, but she did not respond. Dejectedly, I wandered back into the dining room, trying to ignore the stares and whispers of other residents on the way. I sat down to eat my toast and drink my juice. It was then that Murray spoke up.

"Don't worry, Don, she'll come around. Shit happens. She told me just before you came into the kitchen how much she liked you. And don't worry about me; I'm just friends with her– and you."

"Thanks, Murray. I'm glad you told me these things," I said, my hands shaking. I ate my toast, which by now was colder than a three dog night, I thought negatively. I barely remembered even drinking the juice, I was so scared and upset. I said to Murray that I'd see him later, and I went to my room to lay down. I began to Jones out of myself with tears running my head.

The next thing I knew, lunch was being called. I got up rather groggily, surprised that I'd slept for three hours. I was anxious as I walked down the hall looking for Ariel. Instead, I saw her seated at the female residents' table talking to Sandra, an older woman who had lived in the boarding home longer than anyone else. Unfortunately, I had my back to Ariel at my usual place so we couldn't make eye contact. But my first impression was that she wasn't as upset as before when I made my accusation.

I scarcely tasted my sandwich and milk as I counted the seconds left before I could be excused. But Ariel's table was allowed to go before mine, so I missed her in the kitchen as the rest of our table lined up to rinse our plates. I made a bee-line to the medication queue and saw her getting her pills. As she turned down the hall, she looked at me with a strange half-smile. I nodded and beamed my best smile, knowing that she would have given hers, too, if it weren't for the pills in her mouth. I was elated, then a little sad, as I saw her enter the women's washroom. I couldn't believe that the staff weren't on to her palming or cheeking. I was feeling very light again, terrified that Ariel would really Jones out.

I meandered about the halls as I waited for her to come out of the washroom, and when she did, I noticed she had her beautiful, feathery hair down again. I approached her with a smile and asked her if we could talk. To my great relief, she said yes, but not here in the boarding home. She suggested we go for coffee.

" What restaurant do you want to go to?" I asked.
" How about Burger King?"
" Sure," I said.
" Let's get our jackets and go!" she said, her face brightening and her eyes shining like full moons. We were ready within a minute, and as I signed us out on the blackboard, the head nurse Lana told us to go for just coffee, no alcohol. We agreed.

As we left the home, I told Ariel I was sorry for not trusting her, and that I never wanted to upset her.

"I was hurt by what you said, but I'm over it now. I hope you don't mind, but when I was talking to Sandra today she said that you were a nice guy. And I believe her," Ariel said, her eyelashes fluttering above her smile. She hesitated. "Don, do you think you could buy me a pack of smokes, and I'll pay you back on check day?"

I was surprised at her sudden shift in topic, because as a former moderately schizophrenic, I used to do the same thing, which meant that she might be schizo-affective. Or, in other words she might be both schizophrenic and manic-depressive.

"Yeah, I'll buy you a pack, but you don't have to pay me back because I know how hard it is for smokers with our cheap government." At these words, she locked her arm in mine and said she would at least buy me coffee when she got her money. I stopped and kissed her right there, just as an elderly couple walked by mumbling something, but I didn't care. After a minute or so, she pulled away saying that I had a lot of guts to do that. She was breathing heavily.

"It's just that I can't resist you," I blurted, embarrassed, but glad we'd had a powerful effect on each other. We contiued walking, talking about our pasts, particularly our family and school lives. I was almost moved to tears when she told me her parents had died when she was three, and she went to live with her grandmother. But I was surprised when I found out that she had attended UBC for a year. I told her that I was in my fourth year there when I broke down. When I said that only my father was left in my family, she nuzzled her face in the shoulder of my blue coat and sobbed.

"I'm sorry for being so depressing," I said. She looked up, eyes wide as a hungry cat.

"How old are you, Don? I've been meaning to ask. You can't be more than twenty-five." I took this as a deserved bit of a shot for acting a little immature.

"I'm thirty-four. How about you? Or do you mind me asking?"

"That's good. I'm almost the same age. I'm thirty."

I was beginning to understand this wonderfully intelligent woman's mind as we crossed the main street to the restaurant. She had a unique way of saying and finding out things that bordered on being manipulative. But, I was in love. I held the restaurant door open for her, and followed her to a booth.

"What would you like to drink?" I asked.

"Rum and coke. Hold the rum," she joked, and we laughed.

"I'd like to hold yours, all right," I said humourously.

"Why, Don, how dare you!" she laughed, with gleaming eyes.

I got two cokes, and we sipped them slowly in the nearly empty restaurant. We both shared the same dream of going back to school. We also shared similar tastes in literature. Then, she asked me what days I worked at the food bank. I told her just Friday afternoons, which I remembered was tomorrow. By now, I could see that she was leading up to something.

"Don, I spend weekends at my grandma's. I have ever since I got put into mental health. The staff have already arranged for it. I leave Fridays at one and get home Sundays at eight. But I can't stand the thought of us being apart that long. Why don't you come with me? Grandma likes company, and she has an extra room. Would you? Please, for me?" She seemed as lonely and lost like a little bird who'd fallen out of its nest. She stared deep into my eyes, capturing my soul.

"Well, I'd love to, but I don't want to miss work. They need me there."

"When was the last time you didn't go?"

"I haven't missed any time in two years," I replied, somewhat wary of her line of thought. She placed a soft hand on mine.

"I think you need to take time off. You're due for some fun and rest. Please come with me?" she pleaded. I was beginning to feel almost mesmerized, and so I agreed– if the staff would allow me. She reached across the table, grabbed my cheeks which made a fish face, and she kissed me hard.

We finished our cokes and left for the store across the street. My mind was buzzing like flies over her invitation. I barely knew her, but I wanted to be with her. I couldn't bear the thought of the weekend passing by without her. We entered the store and I handed her a five dollar bill for smokes. She ordered them at the counter as I looked at the headlines of the Vancouver Sun newspaper. A few seconds later, Ariel tugged at my sleeve and said she needed another $2.35 because of the GST and PST tax. I reached into my pocket and gave her the money. I didn't know cigarettes were so expensive.

"Do you want me to smoke them for you, too?" I joked.

"Fine! If you're going to be that way about it, I don't want them!"

she complained, as tears began to squirt down her face. She left the store in quite a huff, like a horse coming up on the outside. I gave the storeowner the money, grabbed the cigarettes, and dashed madly through the door to catch up to Ariel. I didn't have far to go: she was sitting by a telephone pole with her face in her hands crying.

"I'm sorry, Ariel, it was a dumb joke," I said soothingly, putting my arm around her shoulders. She shook it off, still sobbing. "Honest, Ariel, I would never mean to do or say anything to hurt you. I love you. And I want to go with you to your grandmother's." I was shocked at what I'd said, not because I didn't mean it, but because I was suspicious that she had orchestrated these events to get what she wanted. Then, a more plausible thought struck me: she was doing these things because she had gone off her medication for a few days. I was becoming aware that her behavior was not always aimed at me. "I love you, Ariel," I repeated.

"Do you really, Don?" she exclaimed, jumping up into my arms, kissing me." Oh, I love you, too! And we can go to my Grandma's together?" Her face by now was glowing with delight. I was solid as a Redwood tree.

"Yes," I said, "and these are yours." I handed her the cigarettes, and we kissed again. When we parted lips, I dried the tears on her gorgeous face with my fingers. We walked hand in hand, discussing how we'd talk to the staff about me going with her to her Grandmother's, both of us excited as children the night before Christmas. We stopped before the boarding home and I looked into her eyes, which were sparkling with the reflection of the sun. *My mistress's eyes are like the sun*, I thought, smiling. *Take that Shakespeare*, I joked inside.

"What are you smiling about, Don?" she said, looking into my blue eyes.

"About being the luckiest guy in the world to kiss you," I said, and we kissed passionately. Then we went around the hedge that led into our home's yard.

We climbed the blue jay colored cement stairs of the sheep white stucco boarding home just as Lana, the head nurse, opened the front door and lit up a cigarette. I knew she wanted to see what we'd been up to and where we'd been. But it was Ariel who spoke first.

"Hi, Lana. Don and I went for coffee, and had another long talk

## The Temptress Ariel

about the two of us spending the weekend at my grandma's. Would that be okay with you? We'll have separate rooms and Don says he needs a break from work. We've got our hearts set on it."

"Well, Don's a big boy and can decide for himself– if it's okay with your grandmother."

"Oh, thank you, Lana! I'll call her right now!" said a gleeful Ariel, as if she'd just won the lottery. I smiled at the two women, although I was slightly embarrassed about being referred to as a big boy by Lana.

"I'll be right back, Don." Ariel said as she disappeared behind the front door.

"Just remember, Don, that Ariel has only been out of the hospital a short while. Try not to rush in over your head," said Lana.

"I thought you said I was a big boy and could decide on my own."

"I did. And you don't have to be sarcastic. I was just offering a little advice."

"I'm sorry. It's just that I care and feel so much for her." Lana's stern frown dissipated into a gentler look. She was about forty with grey hair (most of it I assumed came from dealing with mentally ill people) and she had tree-frog green eyes. She looked out across the street as she puffed on her cigarette.

"I guess you should cancel work for tomorrow today to give them some advance notice." I nodded and went inside. Ariel was just hanging up the phone as I approached her.

"Don! It's okay with my grandma! You can go with me to her place for the weekend!" she chattered like a young schoolgirl.

"That's great!" I said. "I'll phone my work and tell them I can't make it in tomorrow. In the meantime, we'll have to get our meds made up to take with us. Lana and the other nurses like a day's notice to do this. Would you ask her to do that?"

"No, I think we both should," Ariel said determinedly. I sensed a little flak from her so I grinned and agreed to go with her. She smiled that femme fatale smile as I phoned my work. The boss, Ellen, said that I was a good worker and and that I had a day off coming to me. I thanked her for the day off.

"What's your boss like?" asked Ariel when I hung up. I was light but in a relaxed way.

"Oh, she's okay I guess. She's fair and lets people go at their own pace, and if we need a break she's understanding. And she's kind, too. She signs my work record each week so I can get a volunteer incentive check once a month. The people there are all nice and helpful, and I like working there because it's for a good cause."

"Maybe I could get a volunteer job there, too," Ariel said, her big hazel eyes narrowing. I didn't want to discourage her even though I knew she wasn't ready to work, so I told her that I'd look into it soon to see if they needed anyone in the near future. I also thought that she might be a little jealous, but I resolved to give her the benefit of the doubt and assume she was just curious.

We arranged to have our meds made up by Lana, who repeated that alcohol and our medications were dangerous when mixed together. Ariel spoke up, saying that we would just enjoy a quiet weekend with her grandmother, who was not a drinker.

"I know your grandmother, and she's a nice lady. But she can't monitor you two all the time, so please act with maturity and, above all, take your pills at the regular times. Right, Ariel?" Lana looked Ariel straight in the eye as a mother would at a disobedient child.

"Of course we will," said a peeved Ariel.

"No, not we," replied Lana. "Don has never had a problem taking his meds. It's about your meds, because you are still settling in from the hospital and it is very important that you take them. So, keep this in mind and have a good time- within reason." Ariel shot us both an angry glare, like a bear defending territory.

"Fine!" said Ariel, and turned abruptly to walk down the hall. I said thanks to Lana and followed Ariel to her room. I caught up with her just as she opened her door. She turned to me, angrily, and said "What the fuck was that lecture all about? Why does she think I don't take my meds?" She frowned at me. "Did someone tell her I haven't been taking them?"

"So you think I ratted?" I said, pissed off. "Well, I've got news for you: I would never do that or do anything against you. I love you. But you gotta get it into that pretty little head of yours that nurses and doctors aren't stupid- they watch our every move even when we're not aware of them. And if you do fool them, you're only kidding yourself because we need our meds. I wish that you would take your meds, but I won't say anything if you don't. But let's trust each other. I'm not against you, Ariel." She smiled her alluring smile and we hugged. She made me feel heavier again.

## The Temptress Ariel

"I'm going to rest for awhile," she said. "Talk to you later."

I left and went to play music in my room. My mind was full of Ariel, as the music soothed me with its background. My main homing pigeon thought of her was watching her fall apart, and yet I was feeling as powerless as a bird with a broken wing. It scared me, but made me want to care for her and love her even more– the way someone would watch over a wounded or sick little animal until it got better. But perhaps, I thought, I was being a bit arrogant to think that I was her answer. But, I resolved to try to be.

Dinner was called after awhile and I was shocked when Ariel never showed up for it. I squirmed in my seat after barely tasting the spaghetti and meatballs, as I agonized over why Ariel was not there. I raced faster than Secretariat to get to her room once my table was dismissed. I knocked on her door, almost panicking.

Ariel opened her door with a white towel turbanned on her head; she was in her robe and slippers as well.

"How come you weren't at dinner?" I asked. "Were you feeling sick? Was it something I said?"

"Oh, no Don. I just want to lose weight for you by not eating as much. And I want to be clean and fresh for you. That's why I just took another shower for you."

"But Ariel, I love you the way you are. Please don't go without eating. You gotta eat. Okay?"

"Oh, I love you, Don!"

"I love you too," I answered as we kissed and embraced.

"Let's keep it clean, huh kids?" joked Murray as he walked by. Then, I noticed that Sandra was also watching us. I left for my room, as Ariel retreated into her room to do her grooming.

My thoughts swarmed like locusts about Ariel, as I fell into a deep sleep. I was buzzed three times for nine o'clock meds before I got up to get them. After downing my meds, I looked for Ariel in the smoking-room and found her just finishing her smoke; she said she was tired and was going to bed as she walked by me. I asked her what was wrong as I walked with her down the hallway.

"How come you didn't answer me when I knocked on your door about four different times tonight?" she said, somewhat miffed.

"Oh, so that's why you're upset," I said. "Honestly, Ariel, I was so tired from today's outing that I not only didn't hear you, I was buzzed three times for 9 o'clock meds."

"I'm sorry, Don. I guess we both need our rest." Ariel looked tired. "See you in the morning," she said with a wink and a smile. She pecked me on the cheek, and entered her room. I realized that I was still exhausted, so I went to bed too. I fell asleep, almost immediately, dreaming of Ariel.

## ❥❥ Chapter 3 ❦❦

I AWOKE IN THE DARK AND SAW ON MY RADIO ALARM CLOCK THAT IT WAS FOUR a.m. I immediately thought of Ariel and her bright smiling face, as well as the trip to her Grandma's place. I was wide awake now, and anxious. I considered getting a PRN of liquid Haldol; that might help me back to sleep. I rose in my pyjamas, put on my housecoat, and entered the hall with slothfulness.

As I approached the nurses' office, I was surprised to hear Ariel's voice. At first I thought I was hallucinating, but then I heard Colleen, the night nurse, talking to her. I stopped to listen for a second, and heard them talking about me.

Colleen was advising her about safe sex and protection against pregnancy; I couldn't help but overhear them as they talked behind the closed door, but I knocked on the door to do the right thing and make my presence known.

As Colleen opened the door, I saw Ariel look at me in wide-eyed shock and embarrassment. I smiled weakly at Ariel; I was also ashamed for having overheard such personal female talk. Ariel got up and took off down the hall; I could hear her beginning to cry. I turned to go after her but Colleen called me back.

"I didn't mean to overhear anything," I said shakily to Colleen. "I was just coming for a PRN of Haldol. Honest." I was almost in tears.

"It's okay, Don. I know you didn't expect to hear what you did. But

Ariel couldn't sleep and she came to me with some concerns. I can't discuss them with you, although you probably have a good idea what we were talking about. But I wouldn't worry; you're not responsible for the way she feels. I'm sure she'll get over it soon.

"Thanks, Colleen," I said, as she squirted the medication in a blue plastic cup. I drank it, and paused. "Colleen? I guess I'm a little old-fashioned and naive but I would like to be prepared just in case. You know what I mean. I haven't had a girlfriend in so long, and what with AIDS, although I'm not necessarily implying anything will happen...I'm not like that...But, am I making sense?"

"Yes, you are. And I'm glad you're aware that sex should be about emotional and physical safety. But I know you have deep feelings for Ariel. That's why we should communicate and share as much as possible. But by all means be prepared; don't rush things, though."

"Do you find that mentally ill people can succeed in a relationship? I mean, does it happen often?"

"Well, certainly they can, if they're not too ill. Mentally ill people tend to be more sensitive than the average person, if there is such a person. One of the major hurdles you face, and we all do to some degree, is mutual trust. It's hard to open up and be intimate. Give it time."

"Thanks, Colleen," I said, and we hugged. I was beginning to yawn, so I told her I was going back to bed, feeling reassured. I hoped Ariel wouldn't be too upset with what I'd done, but, as I said to myself as I entered my room, I certainly hadn't planned it. I went to bed and was almost asleep when I heard a timid tap at my door.

I got up and opened the door to see Ariel standing in her pink robe and slippers.

"Can we talk?" she asked. I said yes, and turned on the light, and we both sat on my bed. She had been crying, which wrenched my heart. I glanced at the clock, which showed 4:50 a.m. She noticed this, and said rather bitterly that she wouldn't take up much of my valuable time.

"Oh, Ariel," I said, holding one of her dove-white hands, "You are so sweet to forgive me for my airhead mistake, and don't ever think I wouldn't have time for you. I love you." We kissed, and I knew how Joe DiMaggio must have felt when he first kissed Marilyn Monroe. But all too soon, I realized that if Colleen caught us together in my room there would be a big problem. So we reluctantly disengaged and I told Ariel that I would check out the hall to see if Colleen was around. If she was, I would go to the washroom and come out when the coast was clear.

I opened the door, saw that it was safe, and told Ariel. She left, and I patted her rear on the way out. She giggled, smiling that incandescently charming smile over her shoulder. I watched her enter her room.

I went back to bed, my mind swimming with thoughts of Ariel's kisses and her arousing embrace. I wondered what her grandmother would be like, and if she'd see to it that Ariel and I weren't left alone in her place. I was hoping to make love with Ariel, but at the same time I wanted to be respectful towards her and her granny, so I put these thoughts in the back of my mind. I drifted into sleep, and strangely enough began to dream about making love to my ex-girlfriend Sylvia.

The buzzer in my room woke me for meds. I felt refreshed and eager, knowing that I was going to spend a weekend in the company of Ariel. I groomed myself, got dressed, and went for meds. Lana, the head nurse, gave me my meds and asked me how I'd slept. I told her I had needed a PRN last night. She said that it was probably due to the anticipation of going to Ariel's grandmother's. I hadn't really thought of that. Then Lana told me to try to conduct myself with maturity. She said Ariel had a lot of problems, and to be careful and gentle with her. I got the message, I told Lana.

I went into the kitchen hoping to see Ariel, but there was only Chet in there getting a bowl of cereal.

"Chet, have you seen Ariel this morning?"

"Why do you ask?" he said suspiciously.

"I was just wondering ," I said. "No offence, okay?" I was a little antsy that Chet might go off into a paranoid spiel, but fortunately he just muttered that he didn't know where she was.

"Were you going to talk about me, Don?" said Ariel, who had just come into the kitchen behind me. Her beautiful features were marred with anger.

"No, Ariel, I just wanted to see you, honeybunch. I missed you this morning. I'm so happy to see you. And I'm looking forward to going to your grandma's with you."

At these words her anger melted into that smile that made me want to hold her and kiss her right then. But I refrained.

"Would you like something to eat or drink for breakfast, Don?" Ariel asked.

"I'm not hungry, but I wouldn't mind some orange juice. It's sweet of you to offer, my little doll." She made the orange juice and we drank it, talking in low tones in the dining room so Chet couldn't hear us from across the room. We talked until Ariel asked me to join her in the smoking room. I agreed to, but felt reluctant; I didn't like the smell of cigarettes. So we went to the smoking room where just Murray, my friend, was having a smoke.

"Hi, Don. Hi, Ariel. What are you two doing today?" I sensed that he might know that Ariel and I were going to her Grandma's, and I was wondering if Ariel had told him. I felt a twinge of jealousy, but dismissed it as unimportant.

"Oh, we're going to my grandma's for the weekend," she beamed, and I thought that Murray seemed slightly jealous. Ariel lit up her smoke, and puffed. She asked me if I'd ever ridden a horse. She was surprised when I said no, and that I knew almost nothing about them. Murray finished his smoke just then and left the room, wishing us a good weekend. Ariel said there were stables near her grandma's. She said rather sadly that her horse, Teddy, had died in one nearby. Suddenly, she was crying and she buried her head in my chest as I stroked her beautiful hair which felt soft as silk. I kissed her head and she looked up at me, her eyes wide as a frightened cat's.

"I love you, Don." Those words gave me goose bumps, and a rush of passion. I told her I loved her, too. She finished her smoke, while I told her she was beautiful and the only woman for me, the only woman I'd ever want. I was a little surprised, not at my audacity, but because I meant every word. I'd never even complimented Sylvia so earnestly. We kissed and left the smoking room; she said she was going to nap because she hadn't slept too well last night. As she went down the hall I watched her, hoping it was me that had kept her awake and not her lack of medication.

I went into my room and put on a tape, *The Supremes' Greatest Hits*. I was almost shocked when I realized how much Ariel's voice sounded like the golden-throated Diana Ross' voice. I resolved that when the time was right, I would ask Ariel to sing for me. I loved

## The Temptress Ariel

music, and this idea intensified my love for Ariel; I realized I must have sub-consciously put the tape on, having recognized the similarities in their voices. I was also anxious to know if Ariel even listened to and liked The Supremes.

After awhile, I grew tired of playing music, so I wandered into the living room. There was a pool table in the middle of the room, but thankfully no one was playing. I sat down on the brown couch beside Sandra and the Activity Worker, Kim. They smiled at me, and turned back their attention to The Price is Right game show. I was bored and restless, unable to focus on the TV program, so I decided to get a PRN. A commercial came on as I rose, and Sandra suddenly said to me that she hoped Ariel and I had a good time away for the weekend. I thanked her but felt a little intruded upon, if Ariel was telling residents what our private business was. I decided to talk to Lana.

I saw an older resident, Tommy, who was from England, and we both said hello. He wished Ariel and I a happy weekend. I was beginning to feel paranoid that everybody in the house knew about our trip, so I left Tommy in the hallway after excusing myself.

When I got to the nurses' office, the door was closed. I could hear Doctor Parker's voice inside; I remembered that Friday mornings were medication reviews. I would have to wait. I turned around to see Tommy approaching me. He stopped in front of me and whispered to me that as a man of the world, he was always prepared. He said I should be too, and handed me some condoms.

Just as I thanked him, I noticed that Kim, the Activity worker was watching us.

"What are you two doing?" she asked.

"Nothing," I said timidly.

"It's men stuff. Private, you know," answered Tommy.

"Let me see what he gave you, or I'll have to tell Lana and Dr. Parker," Kim stated firmly.

I sighed and produced the packages; Kim said it was a good idea and apologized. She said she had to be sure there were no illegal drugs in the house. I felt embarrassed and begged her not to tell anyone– especially Ariel. She promised.

I went back into my room and flopped like a falling fish onto my bed. I began to cry, but not without realizing that I was afraid of hurting Ariel. Even I could see that my life was beginning to revolve like the Earth around her sunny smile and shining eyes. I somehow fell into a fits-and-starts sleep, dreaming about Ariel not loving me anymore.

I awoke to the sound of lunch being called. I was relieved that I had only been having a bad dream about Ariel. As I entered the long hallway, I saw Ariel ahead of me, going into the dining room. I smiled and said hi to her as I went to sit at my table.

She responded likewise. I noticed the atmosphere seemed a little different, and that I was getting a lot of curious looks. When Chet looked at me with a grin, I knew it was no secret that everyone in the boarding home was expecting some sort of tryst between me and Ariel at her grandmother's. I gobbled my chicken salad sandwich down, ate my fruit salad, and polished off my milk. I scarcely tasted them, my mind was so preoccupied with Ariel.

After lunch, I lined up for pills. Ariel was first in line, and when she got her meds she turned and passed by me with a wink. I watched her out of the corner of my eye as, much to my chagrin, she went into the women's washroom. Suddenly, Lana was telling me that I needed my meds. I held out my hand while she asked me why I was so distracted.

"I guess I'm just a little anxious about the weekend," I said.

"I'm glad you're aware of how you feel," she stated. "And also, I've made up both your medication packs for the weekend. Make sure you take them on time. If you need to talk about anything don't hesitate to call us. I've told Ariel the same thing."

"Thanks, Lana. I guess I'd better go and get ready."

"Be careful, Don."

I went into my room and packed my overnight bag with a change of clothes and hygiene effects. I placed my pills in the bag, and looked at my watch. It was 12:35 p.m. The bus left at five minutes to the hour, so we'd have to leave soon. I opened my door as I was putting on my blue ski jacket while awkwardly holding my carrying bag. Ariel was in front of my door, much to my surprise, talking to Lana. Lana turned to me.

"Please conduct yourselves with maturity and respect. I know Eleanor, Ariel's grandmother, and she will be keeping an eye on you two when it comes to things like alcohol. I know I sound like a broken record, but alcohol and drugs are dangerous to mix with your medications. So have a safe, good time."

Ariel and I agreed with her, and we signed out for the weekend on the blackboard facing the nurses' office.

Ariel looked beautiful in her all-white new clothes: spandex tights, running shoes, and hooded winter jacket. I told her so as we exited the house. She smiled and batted her eyelashes; I noticed she had more make-up on, which I usually didn't like too much on women, but on her it made her look even more gorgeous. Then I remembered to ask her if she ever listened to Diana Ross. When she said yes I was pleasantly surprised, but she also said that most of her ex-boyfriends had asked her the same thing.

I was almost speechless when she told me she used to sing in night clubs several years ago. She sang covers of the Supremes, Aretha Franklin, and Joni Mitchell mostly, she told me. It almost made me feel undeserving of her. I asked her if she would sing for me sometime. She smiled like an angel, I thought, and said yes.

We held hands walking to the bus stop; our bags were slung over our shoulders. When we got there, Ariel lit up a smoke. She puffed for about two minutes until the bus appeared down the street, a few minutes early.

"Oh, shit!" she said, stepping on the remainder of her cigarette. ' The damn bus always seems to come early when you light up a smoke."

I couldn't help but grin, so she punched me lightly on the shoulder, and we boarded the bus. The bus was nearly empty as we sat near the back doors. Ariel said it was only about a fifteen minute ride to her grandma's. We talked about what we would do this weekend; Ariel suggested horseback riding. I was hesitant because I'd never ridden a horse, and also because I knew it was expensive. So I said to her that if she wanted to ride a horse, that would be fine with me, only I'd just watch.

"Don, you don't watch trailriding– you're thinking of English riding. But please, do it for me?" She looked into my eyes, my heart almost melting with love. But I stood my ground.

"If I fell and broke an arm, which would probably happen, our weekend would be shot. But I could always grab a coffee while you went riding, because I know how much you like horses."

"Thanks a lot," she said, her eyes forming tears. "Here's our stop. Let's go, if you still want to."

We left the bus and began the walk down the leaf-strewn sidewalk.

"I love Vancouver in the fall. My grandma's house is just around the corner."

"Ariel, I was thinking maybe we could go to a club and you could sing. We could always drink coke instead of alcohol."

"It doesn't work that way; you don't just walk in and sing. Besides, I don't want to. Just like your not wanting to go horseback riding." She looked angry, but stared straight ahead.

"Well, how about if we discuss it later. After I meet your Grandma."

She nodded, and pointed to an older brown and white split level home.

"Here's my Grandma's!" she said, her mood picking up.

I was anxious about meeting her grandmother, and I hoped Ariel wouldn't throw any scenes while we were there. We walked in without knocking, and we were met by a grey-haired woman who didn't look like she was more than sixty. I was surprised at the tremendous similarities in the two women's facial features. She smiled at me, so I smiled back and offered out my hand.

"Hi, I'm Don. It's nice to meet you."

"Hi, Don. Call me Eleanor. Ariel didn't tell me you were so handsome." I felt a little embarrassed.

"Well, Ariel didn't tell me she had such a young looking grandma," I said, and Ariel and her Grandma smiled.

"Ariel, put your coats and bags up in the closet and come in to the kitchen. I just made some tea. Come into the kitchen, Don."

"Thanks," I said as I followed her down the brown hardwood floor of the hallway.

We entered a bright and cheery yellow-decorated kitchen. I sat down in a yellow-flowery designed swivel chair. Eleanor poured three cups of tea in white-trimmed yellow cups. She asked me if I took milk and sugar. I said just milk, and thanked her. Ariel came in then, kissed her grandma on the cheek, sat down, and began to drink her tea.

"So, Ariel tells me you used to go to college, and now she says you work part-time."

I shot Ariel a glance. "Yes, that's right," I said. "I plan to finish my degree someday. When I've saved up enough money to go back."

## The Temptress Ariel

"I wish Ariel had ambitions like that," she said, coolly looking at her granddaughter. Ariel blushed, and I felt a little resentment at Eleanor's words.

"Well, who knows, maybe she will someday, right sweetheart?" I smiled at Ariel. She smiled back. "Maybe one day we'll both go back together. Or if not, maybe Ariel could make a singing career. Right, sweetie?"

"No!" Ariel said. "No way!" She looked hurt and angry.

"A singing career? Ariel? She's never sang before anyone. Except the time that she auditioned for the night club, Bongo's, and was turned down. What have you been telling him, Ariel?"

"I just told him I sang at a night club. I never said I made any money."

"Now, that's true," Eleanor said. I was becoming uncomfortable with the derision she was aiming at Ariel. But I could also see that Eleanor was letting me know not to believe everything Ariel said.

"You certainly have a nice place, Eleanor," I said, deliberately changing the subject.

"Thank you, Don," she replied. "Oh, by the way, you'll be sleeping in the guest-room downstairs. It has a color TV and a full bathroom; that way you can have some privacy."

I thanked her. Then, she asked me if I'd like to take a look at the room and unpack. I said yes. She said Ariel could help me with it. So Ariel and I rose, having finished our tea, and we took my bag and jacket downstairs.

The room was nicely furnished, with a TV and stereo in an entertainment center, a blue leather couch, a Lazy-Boy recliner, and a queen-size bed. There was a small dresser beside the bed that I put my stuff into. I turned to Ariel, who suddenly began to kiss my face and neck. I kissed her back, feeling the heat of her passion which was like a tigress on a hot day in India. After a few seconds, Eleanor called from downstairs, asking Ariel what she'd like for dinner. We stopped our hugging and kissing.

"Maybe we should let Don decide," Ariel called back, while I shook my head no.

"That's a very nice thought, Ariel. What would you like for dinner, Don?" asked Eleanor.

Ariel was trying not to laugh as I said that Eleanor should surprise us. Eleanor said that was okay, and that she was going to the store. She said she would only be gone ten or fifteen minutes. When we heard the back door close and Eleanor's car start up, we burst into laughter.

Then I put my forefingers on Ariel's breasts, and told her that those were what I wanted for dinner. She laughed and sighed at the same time, which really turned me on. Then we were on the bed, kissing and touching each other. We were acting like rabbits, but before we went too far Ariel whispered in my ear that we'd have to wait for a better time. I agreed.

"I didn't know your Grandma drove," I said suddenly, as we straightened out our clothes. I went into the washroom to see if I had any lipstick on me. I didn't.

"Yeah," said Ariel. "She drives all right. She drives me crazy." We laughed. "But, at least she'll drive us home Sunday night. But during the day she likes me to walk or take the bus because it's good therapy for me."

"Don't you drive, Ariel?" Suddenly her face contorted with pain, and tears appeared on her cheeks. "Did I say something wrong, Ariel, honey?" I tried to hug her but she turned her back towards me. "What's wrong?" I asked, alarmed.

"I had an accident when I was drunk.... it was years....a long time ago....a friend....was hurt...I loved him. He died of cancer two...years ago....his name was Stan. He looked like you.... he was nice like you....but .... that's not why...." Ariel was sobbing.

I placed my arms around her shoulders and chest, kissing her on the neck, telling her it was okay. She turned in my arms, looked me in the eyes, and told me she loved me. I peered deep into her lusty eyes, telling her that I loved her more than any other woman I'd known. I wiped her tears, hoping she would settle down before Eleanor got back, partly because I didn't want her to think I mistreated Ariel, but mostly because it hurt me to see Ariel so upset.

"Maybe we could go to a movie tomorrow," I said suddenly, hoping to pick up her spirits as we left the guest room and climbed the stairs into the kitchen.

"A movie? I don't really like many movies," she said. "Now, if it was horseback riding you wanted to go to, I would gladly go."

"Well, how about if we compromise and go to a movie with horses in it. I'm sure that there must be a good Western playing," I joked. She punched me on the shoulder and said that the joke wasn't funny. Surprisingly, though, she did pick up in mood. I was beginning to realize that her strange behavior was due to a chemical imbalance in her brain, and that my behavior only served as a catalyst for her moods sometimes.

Well, maybe more often than I'd like to admit. But I resolved not to discuss it with her, at least until I got to know her a little better.

## Chapter 4

Eleanor came in through the back door with a bag of groceries, just as Ariel and I sat down at the kitchen table.

"I got us some nice T-bone steaks for dinner, fresh from the butcher's. How does that sound, Don?" Eleanor asked, slightly out of breath.

"That sounds great. I can't remember the last time I had steak. I'm very grateful, Eleanor. Isn't that great, Ariel?"

"Don, it's only steak. You sound like you're starking...I mean.....uh...starving," Ariel blurted out. "Grandma, Don and I want to go out...he doesn't drive...maybe a movie...but not a sad one, I might cry. What I mean....is........is....is it okay, can I have some money?" I looked at Eleanor after Ariel had finished her spiel, and she looked worried.

"Ariel, dear, if you want to go out with Don, the decent thing to do is change those tight white pants. They make you look sleazy. If you do, I'll pay your way into the movies." Eleanor's words sunk my heart. I felt that Eleanor had no right to be so controlling when it was clear Ariel was becoming sick.

Ariel turned away in tears. I followed her down the hallway, but Eleanor called me back, saying that males weren't allowed upstairs. I turned around and walked back into the kitchen. I sat down, trying to repress my anger.

"Ariel will come around, Don. Don't be fooled by her childish games and tantrums. And I know she's off her medication; I was kind of hoping you could help me convince her she needs to take it. If she doesn't, she's headed for the hospital again. I tell you this because I know that you're sensible and that you care a lot about Ariel. You just have to know how to deal with her."

"I see," I said, although I really didn't.

"Good, because that's how she lost her fiance, Stan. He couldn't put up with her mood swings and psychotic behavior. So, I hope you agree that we need to nip this rose in the bud, before she gets out of hand."

"But, this Stan guy, didn't he die of cancer two years ago?"

"Heck no. He broke off the engagement when Ariel's manipulations got to be too hard for him to deal with. Don, don't believe even half of what she says. But, on the other hand, Ariel can be very sweet and loving, even when she's very ill. As a child and young woman, she was hardly ever angry or unhappy. But, as you well know, schizophrenia is a devastating disease. It robs people of the very basics of life."

"So, Ariel is schizo-affective?" I asked.

"Yes, she has been for about five years. She broke down over Stan leaving her." Eleanor got up to turn the kettle off and make more tea. After a few seconds, she handed me a cup of tea as well as three chocolate chip cookies. I scarcely tasted them since my mind was preoccupied with Ariel's relationship with Stan. We sipped on our tea in silence for a minute.

"She told me she broke down over her horse, Teddy," I blurted out.

"Well, that's partly true. Teddy did die around then." Eleanor got up and asked me if I wanted more tea, rather loudly. Then, I heard Ariel coming down the stairs. I was quite certain that Eleanor had heard her before me. Ariel entered the kitchen wearing jeans and a floppy-turtleneck blue sweater. She had brushed her long stream of crow-coloured hair; she was gorgeous. I was relieved to see that she had stopped crying.

"Ariel, you look beautiful," I said. "Doesn't she Eleanor?" I wanted to see and hear Eleanor's reaction to this assessment.

"Well, she looks a darned sight better than she did. But Ariel change that sweater or put on a bra; Don can almost see your nipples.

Aren't you even a little ashamed?" Ariel stomped her foot on the kitchen floor.

"Why do you....always hurt me in front of men I like? You said if I changed......we, Don and me....can go to see the movies. Grandma....you're why I've ....never been married. You...always walk all over me and my dreams." She turned to me. "Don.... do you still love me?"

"How could he love you when he hasn't even known you a week?" Eleanor berated her.

"Not to argue with you, Eleanor, but with me and Ariel it was almost love at first sight." I turned to Ariel. "Yes, I love you, honeybunch."

"Well, I can see you two have your minds made up. If you want to go to the movies, that's fine with me. Besides, it's cold, so Ariel will have to wear a jacket so every sailor on shore leave can't see her breasts."

For the first time I felt intense anger towards Eleanor's derision of Ariel. I changed the subject, hoping to avoid a scene between Ariel and her grandma.

"Where are the theatres from here, Ariel?" I asked, looking at her tenderly.

"Somewhere over the rainbow, I think," Ariel said, looking at the floor.

"You mean The Rainbow Theatre, Ariel," corrected Eleanor. "It's just down the street, Don." Eleanor was beginning to look worried about Ariel. I was afraid for Ariel, too. Eleanor opened her purse and handed us each a twenty. "Have fun, kids." She smiled. I looked at Ariel just as she looked at me, and we both knew that Eleanor was trying to put us in our place. I was certain our eyes spoke volumes about Eleanor's verbal abuse of Ariel– probably abuse that had gone on all of Ariel's life. I wanted to hold Ariel and comfort her, make her feel loved and special.

"Thanks, Eleanor," I said. "You're a great grandmother." Ariel smiled at these words, but Eleanor looked a little indignant.

"Don't forget that supper's at six sharp. So don't go see *Gone With The Wind*."

"Don't worry, we'll be back in time," I said. "Right, Ariel?"

"What?" said Ariel, as she gazed at me. She hesitated. "From the movie?" she asked uncertainly as she put on her white jacket. I put on my coat, too.

"Yes, honeybunch. Let's go. See you later, Eleanor, and thanks for all you've done. Thanks for treating us to a movie. We'll be back by six."

Ariel and I left the house and began the two block walk to the mall where the theatre was. I held her hand and she smiled at me, although her eyes looked a little glassy.

"Thanks for sticking up for me....you know.... in front of my fucking bitch of a Grandma. If you weren't there it would be....have been....a lot worse. I'm sorry, Don, I shouldn't call my grandma names. She's helped me.... and I know that she loves me. It's just that...," Ariel muttered, and burst into tears. I stopped and held her tight, saying I would be there for my honeybunch when she needed me. I told her I loved her.

Ariel looked deep into my eyes, saying she would rather go to the bar near the mall instead of the movies. She said shakily that she needed a drink. I was hesitant and worried because she liked to drink alcohol a lot. Plus, if we went drinking, her Grandmother might give us shit later. Ariel began to plead and whine so much that finally, against my rationale, I gave in.

"Oh thank you, Don!" she exclaimed. "You'll love Bongo's. It's cool." She gave me a quick kiss as we continued walking. We arrived in front of a quaint, old-fashioned looking building. Ariel pointed to its green doors and brown sign that read "Bongo's." I thought that it looked a little like the "Cheers" sign on the TV show. I opened the door for Ariel as we went in.

A waitress inside recognized Ariel, and asked her how she was.

"Oh, I'm fine....this is my new boyfriend, Don.....we came in for a few. Can we have a booth?" The waitress led us to a booth, and asked Ariel if she wanted her usual– a double of rum and coke, neat.

"You read my mind," Ariel laughed. The waitress turned to me.

"I'll have a coke," I said.

"Don, have a drink. Relax. Take your shoes off, and sock one down. Have a little fun, or instead ....have a lot of fun. C'mon," Ariel spieled, but I held my ground. She seemed a bit frustrated.

"Just a coke for me," I stated firmly.

"Okay. And remember Ariel, no nonsense in here," said the waitress. "Or you'll be barred."

"Yeah, yeah," Ariel agreed. The waitress left. I was going to ask Ariel about the nonsense the waitress had mentioned but I didn't want to upset her. Especially since her mood was picking up. We took off our jackets and looked around. The bar was practically empty except for about twenty people. I saw a different waitress walk by. Ariel suddenly looked angry.

"Stop looking at the waitresses, Don. Or am I not good enough for you?"

"I'm not interested in these waitresses or any other woman. I only care for you, honey. Honest."

"I...I'm sorry, Don. You see how badly I need a drink?"

I almost said "You see how badly you need your medication" but I held back, not wanting to upset her. The waitress arrived with our drinks a few moments later, after I had glanced up at the TV screen which was showing wrestling. The waitress left after we paid her, and I noticed that Ariel took a big gulp from her drink.

"I hope you don't like wrestling," Ariel said, a little annoyed.

"Just with you, honeybunch," I said, and we both laughed.

Ariel took such a big gulp of her drink, she was nearly finished it. I began to worry that she might be an alcoholic, as I sipped on my coke.

"That's good, because I hate sports. Except for gymnastics and horseback riding. Hey, maybe we can go horseback riding!"

"We don't have enough money now," I said, hoping to steer her mind away from horseback riding. "Maybe some other time."

"Damn!" she said rather loudly, and finished her drink. "Where's that fucking waitress?" I waved to the waitress, She came over and Ariel ordered the same drink. I told the waitress that I was okay for now with my coke.

"What are we going to tell your grandma about where we went?" I asked, slightly afraid that Ariel would get upset.

"Who gives a shit.... I'm....sorry, Don....but she doesn't own me. I can make up my own face.... I mean, mind. Let's have fun." Ariel looked into her glass, frowning.

I looked at her for a minute or so as she was lost in thought. But when the waitress arrived with her rum and coke, she looked like a child about to open a Christmas present. I was becoming alarmed at the way she was downing her drinks, as she nearly finished her second in one draught.

"Ariel, honey," I said as gently as I could, "I think you should slow down a bit on your drinking."

"What?...I've had only one.... Stan....just because....you don't drink....don't be such a mud in the stick," she retorted, and guzzled the rest of her drink down. Her face contorted as she almost yelled for the waitress. Luckily, no one heard her. "I'm going to sing for you, Stan.....you'll see....and then....you'll be wanting me....hey, that rhymes." She leaned over the table and kissed me. I was aware that she was having the beginning of a psychotic episode. I asked her if she'd like to leave.

"No, Stan," she said, "I want to stay."

"I'm Don, Ariel."

"Okay, Don, I'm Diana. And I'm going to sing one of my songs for you." She rose quickly before I knew what she was going to do. She picked up a microphone on the piano ten feet away, and started to sing Diana Ross And The Supremes' classic song " I Hear A Symphony." She wasn't too bad of a singer but I knew no one would ever pay to listen to her. I got up to stop her from further trouble, but a bouncer suddenly stood between us.

"What's going on here?" he asked me. "We don't want her singing here."

"Hey, take a hike, bimbo!" someone yelled out. Ariel kept singing.

"Shut up, bitch!" a woman shouted.

"She's just a little mixed up," I said to the burly, arm-tattooed bouncer. He confronted Ariel and told her to stop, but she kept right on singing. He grabbed the microphone from her, took her by the arm, handed her off to me, and told me to take her home. As I picked up our jackets, Ariel began to cry. I put her coat on her, and led her out of the bar. The bouncer opened the door and told us never to come back. I said okay, but refused to apologize for Ariel, since she was sick.

"It's okay, Ariel, I'm going to take you to your grandma's," I said.

"Thank you....Stan?" She looked confused and wild-eyed. I held her close to me as she cried, and I walked her home, reassuring her that everything would be all right. I kissed her cheek and soothed her with caresses to her face. Somehow, we made it to her grandma's. She met us at the door.

"Are you okay, Ariel?" she asked calmly. I was grateful for that. Then she looked sharply at me.

"Why was she drinking? I know you weren't– I don't smell alcohol on your breath. I thought you two were going to the movies."

I told her to forget about it, that it was a long story, and that we should just take care of Ariel.

"You're right, Don. Come in, Ariel. I'll make you both some tea." She told me to hold the still sobbing Ariel on the living-room sofa. Then she whispered to me that she was going to get Ariel's medication.

I thought Ariel needed to be in a hospital, or at the very least a psychiatric boarding home, where she could be monitored by professionals. But maybe her Grandmother had dealt with her like this before. I was certain she had, I concluded. I kissed Ariel's strawberry-colored lips and her wide kitten eyes while I waited for Eleanor. Ariel looked into my eyes.

"Stan?" she whispered.

I was hurt. "No, honeybunch, it's Don. And I love you." I kissed her luscious lips, and I wove my fingers through her fine, downy hair. I kept repeating to her that I loved her. It seemed to help, as her sobs lessened. Finally, Eleanor appeared in the door-way. She had our bags and jackets.

"I phoned your boarding home, Solgate, and the nurse told me to take you two home. I explained that Ariel was just mixed up and wasn't a threat to herself or any-one. So, I've got everything; let's go."

I nodded and helped get Ariel up. Eleanor and I helped her into the kitchen, where she placed a cup of tea in front of Ariel. Eleanor placed some pills in Ariel's mouth, telling her to swallow them with some warm tea. Ariel did so, almost mechanically. I watched as Eleanor placed her hand on Ariel's throat and massaged it. This procedure was a little degrading for Ariel, I thought, but nevertheless, it worked. Then Eleanor and I helped Ariel get her jacket on.

I picked up our bags and loaded them in Eleanor's blue Dodge Challenger. Ariel and I sat in the back, as Eleanor started up the car.

"Where are we going....Don?" asked Ariel, looking into my eyes. I kissed her lips, and told her we were taking her home. "Aren't we already home?"

"No, honey, we're going to Solgate instead of your grandma's."

"But I want to stay at grandma's! Please, grandma! Let me stay! Don, I want to stay!" Her face was wet with tears.

"Ariel, dear, you're not well so we're taking you back to Solgate where the staff and Don can look after you. But we'll visit again soon. Everything will be okay," Eleanor said gently. "I love you." She smiled at her granddaughter over her shoulder, reminding me slightly of Ariel's smile.

We sat in silence during the short trip, as I kissed Ariel's mouth occasionally. She looked at me and smiled when I did this. But she looked around her, still a bit confused. Finally, the boarding home loomed, and we pulled into the driveway. I dried Ariel's face with a tissue her grandma handed me.

"We're home, honeybunch," I said tenderly.

## Chapter 5

It was just after four p.m. when Eleanor and I helped a still distraught Ariel out of the car. I was relieved to see that Dr. Parker's car was in the driveway as was Lana's. I knew Ariel would be given the help and attention from them that a mother — or grandmother — couldn't give. As we climbed the low flight of blue stairs, the front door opened and we were confronted by the power of Dr. Parker and Lana. They quickly took Ariel into the office, sat her down, and told me to go to my room. Eleanor went into the office with them as the door closed.

I turned to see some of the residents in the hallway. Murray walked up to me, patted me on the shoulder, and asked how Ariel was. I replied that she was in rough shape, but was being well looked after. I told him that I needed to rest. He said that if I needed to talk about anything, just to ask; he would listen. I thanked him and walked by Sandra and Chet on the way to my room, nodding at them. I went into my room, frightened as a hunted squirrel, and stood looking out the window. Kim, the Activity Worker, pulled up in the house van with several residents, including the Englishman, Tommy. I turned away and plunged, like a seagull into the sea, onto my bed.

I hoped Ariel wouldn't have to go to the hospital; my heart ached at the thought of not being near her. But I chided myself for being selfish: Ariel needed help, and whatever it took would be fine with me. My mind was filled like a photograph with her sweet smile and great beauty. I longed to feel her warm embrace. Suddenly I realized that I was crying, just as there was a knock at my door. I said "come in," as I dried my tears.

Kim, the Activity Worker, entered and asked me how I was feeling.

"I'm very frightened and sad because Ariel is sick. I really hope the Doctor can help her. I don't know.... what I can do.... I feel helpless. But if she needs me I'm going to do my damnedest to be there for her."

"Don, it's very good to see and hear you expressing your feelings about Ariel's health. It will make you stronger and allow you to give her support."

"I feel frustrated about not recognizing what was going on with her. I should have done something."

"Don, you did. Don't punish yourself."

"But, seeing her like that...."

"How did it make you feel?"

"I felt angry and bitter when she wouldn't listen to me."

"How else did you feel?"

"I guess I feel let down and....well....almost cheated. I'm in love with her."

"Why do you feel cheated?"

"Well, I don't know if that's the right word or not– I just want to be with her as much as possible. Not just for sex– I am in love with her emotionally, spiritually, and physically. Well, I guess to be totally honest, I probably love her a little more for her appearance and sweet mannerisms, like most guys would such a beautiful young woman, I guess."

"How do you find dealing with her emotionally?"

"Well, sometimes I feel hurt and upset but for the most part I feel very happy around her. She can be so loveable."

"I'm glad to hear that you have a fairly good handle on this situation. I just wanted to see where you were and discuss how you felt. I'm off work now– it's past 4 o'clock. But, if you need to talk, please by all means feel free to approach the staff. Okay?" Kim smiled and left the room; I felt a little calmer.

I rested until I heard the 5 o'clock call for dinner. I was still obsessed with worry over Ariel as I got up and left my room. I saw Tommy in the hallway, and I asked him if he'd seen Ariel. He said no. So we both walked into the dining room, but Ariel wasn't there. I began to fret that maybe Dr. Parker had sent her to the hospital. When she never came for dinner, I became really worried.

I barely remembered eating dinner and waiting to be excused. I almost bumped into Murray as I tried to quickly rinse my plate, but he told me to slow down and relax, that Ariel would be okay. I thanked him and went for meds.

I was disappointed not to see Ariel in the med line or in the office, but I was even more surprised when Lana, the head nurse, told me Dr. Parker had increased my Clonazepam dosage. She said it was probably temporary to ease my anxiety over the next few days. I wanted to ask how Ariel was, but I knew nurses didn't ordinarily like to be questioned about a resident when other residents were present. So I paced the halls for a few minutes, waiting for the line to dissipate. I smiled at Sandra, Ariel's friend, as she walked by and she smiled back. Then, I approached the office.

Lana was just putting on her coat and talking to Wendy, the evening charge nurse, as I stood in the doorway.

"Lana, I ....was....uh....wondering how Ariel is....and...if....she's still here," I said, shaking slightly.

"She's going to be fine, Don, so don't worry. We gave her some medication, but I would advise that you let her rest tonight. I was just going to tell you this before I left for the weekend. If you have more anxiety and agitation come for a Haldol PRN. Try and relax."

"Thanks, Lana. I was so scared she would have to go to hospital. She'll be okay in a day or two?"

"I would think so. But again, give her space."

"I will."

Lana said goodnight to Wendy and me, and left. I turned and went down the hallway, relieved as a riderless bronco. I saw Murray wave at me, and he invited me into the smoking room. We sat down with Chet and Archie, a very quiet resident, and the three of them lit up their smokes as we began talking.

"Ariel isn't feeling well," I said, testing the waters.

"Yes, I know," said Chet, "she was really out of it when I saw her going to her room. She looked distant and psychotic."

"She's having a schizophrenic episode, I think," said Murray. "What do you guys think?"

"I don't know her," said Archie timidly, looking down through his glasses at his cigarette.

"I'm afraid that I have to agree that she's psychotic," I said.

"Well, don't worry, Don, she'll be okay. I don't think she's gone totally crazy or anything. If she was mad, they would have probably sent her to hospital," said Murray, as the ember on his smoke glowed like an amber traffic light that was changing. I watched him release the puff of smoke from his mouth and I thanked him for his kind words.

The conversation shifted to the Vancouver Grizzlies then, as Archie, Murray, and Chet were going to watch the game at seven p.m. on TV. Murray said that the Grizzlies were hosting the Dallas Mavericks. The game didn't interest me too much as I was still obsessed with Ariel's health. Murray, sensing this, urged me to watch the game with them. So I gave in, hoping for my attention to be diverted for awhile.

I said that I was going to lie down; Murray promised to knock on my door at seven. I thanked him and left the smoking room.

I went into my room and put CBC radio on low, hoping to hear some interesting news, literary readings, or music. But my thoughts were filled with Ariel like a sated lion's stomach as I tossed and turned on my bed. I knew that I was deeply in love with Ariel to the point of obsession, since my thoughts revolved around her like an eagle circling to protect its aerie. I smiled as I thought of the word "aerie," and how close it was to "Ariel." Freud would have had a field day with these words and thoughts. I thought that his theories would suggested that the aerie/Ariel nest symbol was about the vagina. Ariel's.

I sat up suddenly, trying to drive these bizarre ideas out of my head. I heard a voice say "Listen to your mind and be free." Then another voice said "You don't deserve her, you drove her crazy, drop her." I began to panic a bit, since I hadn't heard demonic voices for several years. I realized that I needed a PRN to prevent the voices from overwhelming my mind. I got up and went to the nurses' office.

I appeared in the doorway of the office and asked Wendy for a PRN of liquid Haldol. She looked at me and asked me how I was feeling and why I wanted some extra medication. I told her I was hearing voices because I was afraid for Ariel, and that the stress of the last few days was catching up to me. She said it was good that I understood that voices were symptoms of my illness, which had flared up due to stress. She gave me the medication and told me to try to relax.

I turned and saw Murray coming down the hallway.

"The game starts in ten minutes, Don," he said. "You okay?"

"Yeah, I'm all right. Thanks, Murray."

"I bought a six pack of coke and two big bags of potato chips for the game. So let's go pig out to our heart's content," grinned Murray. This sounded good to me, since we seldom had the luxury of such treats; we were both over two hundred pounds with big stomachs and elephant appetites.

"Sounds great, Murray."

"We're watching it downstairs in the Rec Room so we won't be disturbed by anybody playing pool. I like the Grizzlies team this year, especially with Shareef, our favorite player. See you down there in five minutes. I'm just going to get our tasty treats for the game."

I paced the halls for a few minutes until my head cleared up from the voices. The thought of watching the basketball game interested me, so I went downstairs. The game was just starting. Murray handed me a can of coke and a small bowl of chips as we settled down to watch the Grizzlies. Chet and Archie were more vocal than I'd ever heard them, especially when Shareef Abdur-Rahim scored for the Grizzlies. We had a good time cheering our team on until nine o'clock, when meds were called.

We waited for a commercial, and then stormed upstairs for meds. I was last in line. When my turn came for meds, I smiled at Wendy as she gave me my pills, but I was shocked with delight to see Ariel sitting in the office, looking much better. I beamed at her, asking her how she was.

"I'm fine, Don. Thanks for being so kind and caring."

"If there's anything I can do for you, I'll be there. Just ask," I said, relieved to see her in much better shape, although she still looked tired. She gave me one of her pretty smiles.

"I'm going to bed after I finish talking with Wendy," Ariel yawned. "Sorry. I'm just so tired. I've been sleeping all day."

"That's okay. Just get better, that's the main thing," I responded. Wendy asked me how the game was going. I thought I was interrupting them, so I apologized and said it was great, and that I should be getting back to it. I said good night to Ariel as I left the office. She smiled and winked, wishing me a good night too. Happily, I went back downstairs to join the guys watching the game.

"We're ahead in the game," grinned Murray.

"So am I," I said. "I just saw Ariel, who's doing much better."

"That's good," said Murray, as we all chuckled. We watched as the Grizzlies held on to their lead and won. We whooped it up a bit and high-fived our hands at the end of the game. The guys said they were going for a smoke; I told them that I was going to bed.

I got undressed and hopped into bed. Voices hadn't come back after the PRN, but I knew that the main reason for their leaving was seeing my beloved little angel, Ariel. I turned the radio on low and drifted off to sleep. I began to dream that Ariel and I were married and had children. But the dream was interrupted when I heard a light knocking on my door. I looked at my clock: it was 1:30 a.m. I rose and opened the door in my pyjamas. It was Ariel in her pink housecoat.

"Can I come in, Don?" she asked with that winning smile. She was looking as chipper and charismatic as ever. "The nurse is downstairs doing the cloth laundry. All the other residents are asleep. I thought we could....you know....communicate."

"Yes, honeybunch, let me show you in." I was ecstatic. The next thing I knew I was holding her and kissing her. I led her under the covers of my bed, and we began to fumble with each other's bed clothes. She sighed as I kissed her breasts and neck.

Then, somehow, she had a condom, and she slipped it on my erection and we began to make love. She giggled and sighed as I began to moan. She covered my mouth with hers as I came inside her. The old story about the two flowers that almost became one had finally been realized, I thought. We caressed each other for awhile, speaking in low tones. Then she kissed me on the mouth and said she had to go back to her room.

"How about if I do what I did the other night and go to the washroom to see if the coast is clear? That way we won't get caught."

She said yes and smiled while we got dressed again. I kissed her rose petal lips and walked into the hall. The nurse was in the office because the door was open. I went and told Ariel that the coast was clear.

She left my room just as Sandra came out of a room down the hall. She was half asleep, but I was fairly sure she knew what Ariel and I had been doing.

"Thanks for lending me that book, Don. It was a good read," Ariel said so that Sandra could hear. "See you tomorrow." Ariel went back to her room, as Sandra gave us a strange look and went into the women's washroom.

I went back to my room with depressingly mixed emotions. I wanted to ride high on the love Ariel and I shared, yet I was afraid of Sandra ratting us out. I resolved to think only pleasant thoughts of Ariel and me, only caring to be with my love. I would love her no matter what. I fell asleep slightly reassured. I began to dream that Ariel and I were loving rabbits, and that she was my honey-bunny.

# ❧ Chapter 6 ☙

I woke at the buzz for meds, Ariel's sweet love still strong in my mind and body. I craved to see her, to touch her, to kiss her. I knew I was madly — almost literally — in love with her, like a stallion with his mare, I thought. But as I rose, I focused myself on not being too possessive and obsessed with Ariel, although deep down I knew I was a mule who'd kick whatever problem came between us.

I opened my door and was delightfully surprised to see Ariel coming down the hall, her eyes shining like embers. And I was her match, I thought, as I said good morning to her.

"Are you going for meds?" she asked, as I looked around the hall to see if anyone was watching. I kissed her quickly, and said yes.

"Don, not here," she said, giggling and pulling away.

"How about here, then?" I laughed, as I hastily felt her small but sexy round breasts. Just then, Murray came out of his room, glimpsing Ariel and I looking at each other.

"Hey, let's keep it clean, huh kids?" He teased.

"I was just giving her her physical," I joked, but Ariel punched me on the shoulder lightly, which meant she was both pleased and a bit hurt by my flippancy. Murray grinned as he went by, and I told my precious little lamb Ariel that I would try to be more discreet. She smiled at this and said she'd make me breakfast after she showered.

"Did you get your meds?" I asked her, just as Sandra came around the corner.

"Yesterday," Ariel said, plunging me into a sea of panic.

"Yesterday?" I said, as we nodded at Sandra passing by. Sandra nodded and smiled. She went into her room, humming Elvis' "Love Me Tender."

"It's okay, Don. They gave me a shot of Fluphenazine. It lasts for two weeks. I only take Lithium before bed– like last night when you saw me in the office. I want to get better for you."

"You're such a sweetheart to say that, honeybunch." I smiled, as relieved as an ox released of its yoke. She smiled her enticing smile over her shoulder as she went and entered her room, hesitating long enough to blow me a kiss from her siren-red lips. I turned to go to the nurses' office to get my meds.

There was only Chet in line when I arrived at the office. I suddenly remembered that Sandra had seen Ariel come out of my room last night, and I hoped that she hadn't told the staff. But I got my meds without any questions about last night. The nurse, Barb, asked me how I was feeling as she gave me my pills, and I grinned and told her that I was fine.

I left the office in a good mood and saw Emma, the weekend Activity Worker, who told me it was time to shower, and that she'd check it off when I was finished. The boarding home required a minimum of one shower every two days for each resident.

After I showered and dressed, I eagerly went into the kitchen where I saw Ariel making scrambled eggs and bacon. She was talking to Murray, who was making toast.

"It's ready, Sandra!" Ariel stated loudly, and Sandra came into the kitchen and accepted her breakfast plate. "There you go, dear," Ariel said to her.

"Hi, honeybunch," I said to Ariel, who turned around while Sandra and Murray looked at us, amused.

"Hi, sweetheart," Ariel replied. "Your breakfast is in the microwave oven, covered up. You just need to heat it. Try about forty-five seconds. I'd do it for you but I'm busy making Murray's breakfast."

I felt a twinge of jealousy at Murray getting more of Ariel's attention, but I shook it off. I turned the microwave on to a minute, because I liked my food quite hot.

"How's it going, Ariel?" asked Emma, coming out of the dining

## The Temptress Ariel

room with an empty plate and glass. "Do you need any more help?" Each staff member was allowed one free meal a day, so obviously Emma had decided on breakfast.

"I'm fine," answered Ariel.

"You're a good cook, Ariel. Have you ever worked in a restaurant?" asked Emma.

"No, I haven't worked in a restaurant. My grandma taught me how to cook."

Ariel began to assemble Murray's food on his plate, and I couldn't help but feel relieved when he handed Ariel two cigarettes. I turned at the sound of the beeping microwave. I felt the plastic over the food and it was nice and hot. I thanked Ariel and went into the diningroom and sat across from Murray. Ariel joined us, supplying three cups and a pitcher of orange juice.

We thanked her as she poured the orange juice into each cup. Then, I asked her if she'd already eaten. She said no, that she was on a diet. I told her that I didn't think she needed to diet; Murray also agreed with me.

"But what if I get fat, Don?"

"You won't. And even if you did, there would just be more of you to love," I responded with a wink and a grin.

"Oh, Don, it is so sweet of you to say that!" Ariel leaned over the table and kissed me on the mouth.

"Maybe I should leave," joked Murray as we all laughed. Then, Emma came into the dining room and told us to just concentrate on eating our breakfast, and to have no more kissing. She turned and left.

"It feels like we're living in 1984, not 2000," I joked. "And not Van Halen's 1984, but George Orwell's 1984." We all laughed.

"Maybe she was Hitler's long-lost daughter," grinned Murray, and we again laughed. Needless to say, the part-time Activity Worker was not well-liked compared to the rest of the staff. She was a power tripper.

"Maybe her name should be Enema because she's always giving us shit!" I joked, and we roared like hyenas.

"Oh, you guys are bad," laughed Ariel. "Is Emma really that arrogant?"

"You don't know her like we do," said Murray. "She can be a little mean at times."

"I usually try to steer clear of her," I said.

We finished our breakfasts in silence. Then Murray suggested that the three of us could go for coffee, his treat.

Ariel and I agreed, and we took our plates into the kitchen to rinse them off. As we were doing so, Emma and Barb came into the kitchen. Barb said that there was going to be a trip to Stanley Park in the van with Emma, and that if we were going she'd need to make up our after-lunch medication packages. Emma said that if we went we'd be stopping somewhere for coffee as well. The payment for coffee would come out of the Recreation Fund. She needed to know if we were going, so that she'd know how many lunches to make.

"We were just getting ready to go for coffee," said Murray.

"Well, you can have coffee on the outing," replied Emma. "Remember, part of living here is being involved in house activities. I would strongly advise you to come with us. Chet and Sandra are already signed up to go with us. And Tina, the nurse, will be coming, too."

The three of us agreed to go, and we were informed by Emma to be ready in twenty minutes. The weekend cook, Diane, came into the kitchen just then and said she'd make the lunches. I was pleased when Ariel offered to help her; it was another sign that she was feeling better, I realized.

Murray and I left the kitchen and went into the living room. I collapsed into a LAZ-Y boy recliner and sighed. Murray sat on the sofa to my right.

"You seem disappointed that we're going to Stanley Park. I'm looking forward to it; plus, I think it'll be good for Ariel. It should be fun. And we get a free coffee."

I respected what Murray said because he was a smoker, and mentally ill people who smoked were almost completely impoverished, so a free coffee meant a lot. But I also knew that Murray was thinking we would have a good time away from the depressing boarding home.

"Yeah, Murray, I think you're right. Anytime spent with Ariel is more than worth it to me. I'm glad you're going too."

"Can I tell you something, and you promise not to tell anyone here including Ariel?" whispered Murray, looking around the deserted living room.

"I think so," I mumbled, hoping that it wasn't anything bad about Ariel.

"I have a crush on Tina, the new nurse. I think she's warm, kind, caring, and cute. I trust you not to tell anyone."

"Don't worry, Murr, I won't tell. But if all goes as planned maybe someday the four of us can go on a double date." We both grinned.

"She can't be more than twenty-five, and I know she's single. But, to be honest, I think it's a lost cause for a lonely schizophrenic."

"Hey, you never know, Murr. Look at me and Ariel. I would've never dreamed that I'd fall so madly— excuse the expression— in love. And she loves me back. Life's always a new game each moment— we just never know what can happen, especially when it comes to relationships. I never knew how great it was to be in love. So don't give up without trying."

"Yeah, but she's staff," said Murray, somewhat dubiously.

"So, she's human, too. And she wouldn't be working in mental health places if she wasn't interested in people like us. I'll keep an eye on her to see how she reacts towards you. But I promise I won't tell Ariel. Okay?"

Chet came out of the smoking room just then and asked us if we were going on the outing. We said yes. I was surprised when he said he had been watching the weather channel on TV earlier and it said that the high today would be 12 degrees Celsius.

"That sounds cool," Murray joked, and we all laughed.

"Well," I said, "I guess we ought to get ready and dress warm." We went down the hall past Archie who was talking to himself; he was really sick today. As we walked by him towards our rooms I glanced at Murray, who looked worried for Archie. I knew they were good friends. I felt a little sad as I went into my room and opened a brown dresser drawer to get a heavy sweater. I chose a grey kangaroo jacket and put it on. Then I got my blue coat, and I left to sign out on the board by the office. Murray was there, talking to Chet and Emma.

"I already signed us out on the trip," said Murray, and I thanked him. Then Tina, Sandra, and my gorgeous Ariel came out of the kitchen with a couple of baskets of food, drinks, and other items. Murray and I offered to carry them out to the van; nurse Tina gave Murray a big smile as he relieved her of the basket. Ariel handed me the other basket as we unabashedly beamed at each other.

We left the house with excitement building slightly in our group. I followed directly behind Ariel like a faithful puppy, hoping I could sit beside her in the van. We filed singly into the van, with Tina pulling double-duty as driver and therapist. Emma sat in the front seat beside her, while Ariel and I sat in the back seats together. I was mildly surprised when she put her gloved hand in my hand. I looked deep in her eyes, longing to kiss her, but I held back. She tilted her head a little and smiled as she fluttered her eyelashes like a butterfly's wings.

"I'm glad we're going together, hon," I whispered to Ariel. "You mean the world to me."

"Oh, Stanley....I mean Don— sorry, my love— I'm glad we're going to....uh....the park together. Please don't be offended," Ariel said softly, "I'm still a bit mixed up."

"Oh, Ariel," I said softly, "you don't have to explain. I understand you're still not feeling well."

She smiled and squeezed my hand with her black leather glove. But I was hurt again by her confusing me with Stan. Or perhaps she was thinking of Stanley Park. I doubted that, but let it ride.

In the meantime, Emma had been talking about what parts of the park we'd be visiting. It's doubtful if anyone heard her because I was enamored of Ariel, Murray was watching Tina while she drove, and Chet and Sandra had extremely short attention spans. She asked us if we had any questions.

"Will we be going to the zoo?" I asked.

"Don, were you not listening? I just said that was where we were going first. And I repeat that we must stay together. If you feel uncomfortable there, let either Tina or me know. But I think we'll all have fun."

We spent the rest of the trip looking out the windows at the people and traffic. I thought to myself that the residents on this trip were the most stable in the house. But my mind kept reverting back to Ariel, who was watching Vancouver's jungle of high-rise buildings clog around us as we entered the downtown core. I was hoping to spend some time alone with her, but I knew Emma would be keeping her eyes peeled. Emma Peel, the Avenger, I joked to myself about the old British TV show. I inadvertently smiled.

"What are you smiling about, Don?" asked Ariel suddenly but quietly.

## The Temptress Ariel

"About how happy I am with you."

"You're sweet." I squeezed her gloved hand. Then, I noticed Murray was having a chat with Tina as he sat directly behind her. Tina seemed to be quite interested in what they were talking about–whatever it was.

"Don....why are you looking at Tina?" Ariel asked, removing her hand from mine. "Do you still love me? You're acting different. What's wrong?"

"It's okay, hon, I was just noticing that Tina likes talking to Murray."

"So why should that concern you?"

"Murray's my friend. It's okay. Really."

She smiled her winning smile and rested her head on my shoulder. Her flow of feathery black hair smelled wonderful.

"What's going on back there?" demanded Emma, who was watching Ariel and me.

"Nothing," I said, "Ariel is just a little tired." I put my arm around Ariel's shoulders in defiance. "She just needs some rest. You know me, Emma, it's okay."

"It's okay, Emma," said Tina, interrupting. "We're not living in the Middle Ages. Don and Ariel are an adult couple and they're not doing anything wrong."

"I was just checking," backtracked Emma.

We sat silently for the rest of the trip, until Vancouver's famous park came into view. I looked at Ariel, who had somehow fallen asleep. I wondered if it had anything to do with our being together last night. I hoped so, as I sneaked a kiss to the back of Ariel's head, just as the van approached the zoo parking lot.

# Chapter 7

We piled out of the van, and Emma told us to stay in a group. We left the food in the van and Tina locked the doors, smiling at Murray, who was standing next to her. Ariel tugged at my sleeve, yawning, but looking a little hurt. I grinned at her and patted her tight, white-spandexed rear when no one was looking. She smiled at this, her mood rising dramatically.

Tina said that we would visit the zoo first, which was just a few hundred feet away. Ariel and I were suddenly holding hands, which Emma noticed, but didn't say anything since Tina didn't seem to mind. We walked slowly through the autumn leaves on the ground, beneath the leaf-shedding trees, mostly maple ones. There were a few squirrels scampering around us looking for food and preparing for Vancouver's relatively mild winter.

We watched the bears first. The polar bears were swimming, and when they dove into the water the crowd oohed and aahed. Ariel was having a good time, I noticed, watching these giant half-ton bears.

"It's a good thing we didn't bring our pic-a-nic baskets here. Yogi there might have taken them," joked Murray, and we all laughed at his slightly psychotic humor. Next, we went to see the penguins, who were very active. We watched them waddle, preen, swim, and dive for fish.

"Where's Batman?" Murray joked, and again we laughed.

"I don't know, but you must be The Joker," I quipped, and we laughed once more. Ariel was very amused by our humor, and locked her arm through mine. We continued on, looking at the ducks, geese, and seagulls that were all over the park, it seemed. We looked at some of the other animals including monkeys, snakes, and whales. Ariel held very close to me when we looked at the snakes, so I put my arm around her shoulders and whispered in her ear that it was okay, I was there. She gave me a quick kiss, which I liked, but I noticed the sour-minded Emma looked at us with disapproval.

We looked at the statues and monuments until we got to the kangaroos, which were jumping about.

"If those kangaroos became psychotic, they'd be hopping mad," joked Murray yet another time. We all chuckled.

"Murray, I've never seen this side of you," said Tina. "You're very witty. It's good to see you in such a playful mood."

"Thanks," replied Murray.

We continued walking, looking at the snow-hatted mountains to the north of Vancouver. Finally, we arrived back at the van just a few minutes before noon. Murray and I carried the picnic baskets to a picnic table as Tina locked up the van. She gave us our meds with cups of orange juice as Emma passed out the food, reminding us to beware of seagulls because they sometimes take food right out of people's hands.

After lunch, we walked a little way of the seawall, dwarfed by Vancouver's skyline. The harbor contained many freighters. Ariel seemed to be enjoying herself, and would occasionally flash that seductive smile at me. I wished we were alone so we could hold and love each other.

Ariel began to tire noticably, so Tina decided to cut the trip short. We walked back to the van and climbed in, with Ariel and me in the rear seats again. She leaned her head on my right shoulder. I whispered to her that I loved her. She smiled like a sleepy cat.

"Are you okay, Ariel?" asked Tina as she drove the van out of the parking lot.

"Yeah," Ariel answered, but I noticed her eyes were becoming very glassy. I was worried.

"Do you feel up to going for coffee or would you rather go home?" Tina queried.

"Coffee's good....yeah....I don't know....whatever." Ariel sat up all of a sudden.

"Try to decide, Ariel," interrupted Emma.

"Teddy!" She yelled at the top of her lungs. "Stan, what are you doing on my Teddy!" We all looked to see a policeman on a horse, riding on the side of the road. "Get off of Teddy!" she screamed hysterically.

I held her with my arms around her chest so she couldn't get out of the van. I was alarmed at how quickly Ariel had become psychotic.

Tina began to speak to the police officer, and he called for an ambulance. Ariel began to sob in my arms as I soothed her, stroking her hair.

"Teddy....Stan....don't leave me....don't leave me," she repeated softly.

"It's okay, Ariel, Don's here and I love you. Stan's gone, so it's you and me, honeybun," I said reassurringly, hoping to make her forget Stan.

She looked up at me through her tears and painfully contorted face.

"Don?" she whispered, "where are we going?"

"We're going to a place where you can sleep and rest," I said, my heart almost breaking, seeing her like this. The ambulance arrived a few moments later, and Emma accompanied Ariel in the ambulance which set out for the hospital. Tina asked Chet, Sandra, and me if we were all right. I was a little ashamed that I hadn't thought about how Chet and Sandra were feeling, but they answered that they were fine. So did I.

"Do you guys still want to go for coffee?" Tina asked.

"Yes," said Chet, echoed by Sandra.

"Okay, I guess," I said, hoping to ease the pressure of worrying about Ariel.

"Then we'll go. How does Burger King sound?"

We all said great.

So Tina maneuvered through the busy downtown traffic while we sat silently, all of us hoping that Ariel would get better soon. We stopped at a Burger King somewhere in Surrey, a large suburb of Vancouver. We went inside and we all sat in a booth. Tina took our orders, and it didn't surprise me that we all wanted a hot chocolate, including Tina. Tina asked me to help her carry them back from the counter, and I gratefully said yes, knowing she was trying to divert my attention away from Ariel.

We drank our hot chocolates in silence, but I didn't remember tasting mine. I became aware that Tina was saying something to me, but I was hearing Ariel's voice coming out of her mouth.

"I love you ,too, Ariel," I said to her.

"Are you okay, Don?"

"Of course I am, honeybunch. I love you."

"I'll be right back," said Tina. "Keep an eye on him, will you, Murray?"

Tina, I was told later, phoned an ambulance for the second time that day. By the time she got back, everyone's face in the restaurant looked demonic or had an animal head. I was remotely aware of talking to myself and the evil beings. They had taken my Ariel away again, as two men took me into an ambulance. I began to cry. The ambulance guy tried to calm me, but I was becoming hysterical. I was terrified of losing Ariel to Stan.

I was admitted to the hospital, bawling my eyes out unabashedly, as the song goes. I recalled a blur of white and a needle going into my arm. The next thing I knew it was morning, and I was observing four golden spaceships hovering above the north shore mountains. I began to call out for someone to see them; a nurse came in right away.

"Did you see the spaceships?" I said excitedly, as they disappeared.

"No, but I was close by to make sure you were all right," she said.

"Am I under surveillance? Like cameras from the FBI and CIA?" I asked, frightened. "Are you a spy?"

"Don, there are no spaceships or spies after you. You have a brain disease called Schizophrenia. Come and get your medication."

I put my housecoat on as demons whispered in my ears not to trust or tell these people about them. I followed the nurse to the nurses' station and held out my hand for pills. They were different than my regular meds. I asked the nurse who gave them to me and what they were. She said Olanzapine and Ativan. I was suspicious.

"Did the government order this?" I asked. "What the fuck is Olanza- whatever. Why has my medicine been changed?"

"Don, if you don't calm down, we'll put you in the quiet room."

The nurse hesitated as I became more collected. Pleased that her words had had their intended effect, she told me to go for breakfast.

I went down the hall with Angela, the nurse I had met first. I asked her where I was and what day it was. She told me I was in Surrey Memorial Hospital's psychiatric ward and that it was Sunday morning. She told me to try to relax and let the pills and therapy help me get better.

I entered the day room where about twenty patients were eating. I got my tray and sat down at a table beside a young woman, while Angela sat across from us.

"You look like Luke Skywalker," the woman said to me.

"Really?" I answered, somewhat flattered, although I couldn't figure out why.

"Are you?" she asked seriously.

"Maybe in a parallel universe," I replied. "Anything's possible."

The nurse looked at us with slight disapproval, and told us to finish our bacon and eggs. We did so without another word, and put our trays back on the mobile racks. I told Angela that I was going to rest. She said that that was a good idea. I went into my room and flopped on my bed like a pouncing cat.

I began to dream of a woman who I knew I loved, but I couldn't quite place when and how. She had long, crow-feathery hair and was slightly plump and just a bit over five feet tall. She was the most beautiful woman I had ever seen. Who was she? I kept wondering. Then, a demon on a horse rode by and picked her up and took her away. It was Satan. I began to yell for him to bring her back. Suddenly, Angela the nurse was there telling me that I'd just had a bad dream. I looked around my room groggily, and told her about my dream.

"What would you do if you met this woman again?" asked Angela tenderly.

"I would tell her I love her. But I don't remember her name. But she's real; I know it."

"Well, it'll be lunch in half an hour, so maybe you can wash up and get ready for it." She smiled and left my room.

I decided to pace the halls and get my bearings in this psychiatric ward. I nodded to several people who smiled and told me not to worry, that this was a good place. As I passed the large, glassed-in nurses' station, it seemed that the nurses were watching me intently.

I looked ahead and saw the two seclusion rooms; a face was peering out of one, babbling about something. As I got closer, I realized it was the woman in my dreams. I moved right up to the glass, ecstatic.

"Stan, it's Ariel!" she shouted. Then it all came back to me. My love affair with Ariel. I turned to see Angela by my side. I began to cry, and Angela led me back to my room.

"Was that really Ariel?" I whispered through my tears.

"Yes, Don, and I'm sorry you had to see her like that. She's not very well."

"But, I still love her," I sobbed as Angela put her hand on my shoulder.

"I know, Don, I know," she said soothingly.

## Chapter 8

After what seemed like a turtle's eternity, I stopped crying. Angela told me it was lunch time and medication time as well, as she stood and offered her hand. I took it and thanked her. I noticed for the first time that I was in my pyjamas and had on a different housecoat than at Solgate, the boarding home. But, I was worried about Ariel, and I mentioned my concern to Angela, who was fairly tall, young, and pretty with chick-colored hair and ocean-blue eyes. I felt a little ashamed for not noticing her before and then for noticing her now.

"Ariel will be fine, don't worry. You need to take care of yourself first," said Angela as we walked out of my room and down the hallway into the dayroom for lunch. I found my tray, after noticing that most of the patients had already eaten. Angela sat across from me as I ate my lunch. I looked up occasionally to see if Ariel was around, in the long-shot hope that she had been released from seclusion.

Finally, I finished and Angela went with me to get my meds. I got in line, as Angela said she was going into the nurses' office and for me to call her if I needed anything. I thanked her. Then, I noticed on the blackboard in the hallway that each nurse had three patients designated for their shift. I was surprised when I saw under Angela's name, Ariel's name and mine along with someone named Dale.

"Excuse me, Don," said a friendly female voice. "Here's your medication." I turned to see a grey-haired, rosy-complexioned nurse smiling at me, holding out my pills in one hand and a blue med-cup in the other.

"What is it?" I asked.

"Just what Dr. Hilton ordered. Olanzapine and Luvox. Here you go."

I took the pills and swallowed them; Luvox always left a bitter taste in my mouth, but I noticed Olanzapine was almost tasteless. I turned down the hallway and proceeded towards the seclusion rooms. There was no one in either window, so my hopes soared like a rising eagle. Maybe Ariel was out of seclusion, I dared to think.

I wandered into the TV room and looked at the sad and frowning faces watching some courtroom show; I left immediately, dismayed that Ariel wasn't there. I also noticed that the patients' phone was in the TV room, which I thought might cause trouble if someone got too loud. I headed back towards the dayroom.

I saw a man of maybe forty making tea on the counter in the dayroom. I asked him if I could have some too. He smiled and said yes.

"My name's Don," I said, offering my hand.

"I'm Dale," he said. His handshake was very strong. "What are you here for?"

"Minor Schizophrenia– I lost my girlfriend and went a bit out of control. Hearing demons....but I'm okay now," I stated.

"You're doing well, considering. I bet you'll be out of here within a week. Me, I tried to off myself by taking an overdose of pills, but my mother caught me. I was lucky I wasn't sent to Riverview."

He seemed sad, and his face was haggard, probably after years of mental illness. He handed me a cup and poured my tea. I thanked him. He poured himself a cup, and we sat down at an empty table.

"Have you met a woman named Ariel in here?" I asked. "She lives in the same boarding home as me."

"Yeah, I have, actually. About ten minutes ago. She was in the smoking room. She had just gotten out of seclusion, and was having her first smoke in two days. She said she'd been trying to quit for her boyfriend but ended up getting totally stressed out."

"I see," I said, trying not to frown. "Thanks, Dale. I'll talk to you later." I rose as quick as a guard dog and headed for the smoking room.

"Don! Your tea!" Dale called.

"I'll have it later," I replied over my shoulder. I stepped into the hallway by the smoking room door and almost bumped into Ariel, who was coming out of the smoking room.

"Don!" she shouted. "It's so good to see you! I was just going to look for you....my grandma is here visiting.....I saw you in seclusion... I didn't mean to call you Stan. I was sick."

We both began to cry as we hugged each other.

I kissed her neck, and then we were separated by Angela. She said there was no love-making in the ward. Eleanor was also there and agreed with the nurse. But I was happy to just be around Ariel.

"Can we have a cup of tea together?" I asked with a bit of underlying sarcasm. "That wouldn't be breaking the rules, would it, Angela?"

"Of course not, Don," said an irked Angela.

"Well, I'm going to be meeting with Dr. Hilton briefly, and then I'm leaving. But I'll visit you again tomorrow, Ariel. Goodbye, dear, and behave. Good-bye, Don, and keep a close eye on Ariel," Eleanor said and left with Angela towards the doctor's office.

"Are you okay, Don?" Ariel asked, her eyes sad as a motherless kitten's.

"Yeah.... I was just worried about you....you don't have to quit smoking for me. I love you. Let's go get some tea." I wanted desperately to hold her, kiss her, feel her breasts, but I held back, even when she gave me one of her most charming and seductive smiles.

"Thank you, Don," she said as we entered the dayroom.

I put the kettle on and I noticed Dale still drinking his cup of tea.

"Your tea's cold, Don, so you can heat it up in the microwave if you want," advised Dale.

"No thanks, Dale. I'm having a fresh cup with my girlfriend, Ariel."

Ariel radiated with happiness at these words.

"I guess we both can't live without each other," said Ariel. "I loved Stan once, but I'm over him now. I only love you, Don."

"I thought Tina was you and I called her Ariel, but I was sick too, hon. I hope you can forgive me." I didn't want to tell her this so soon but I was afraid that someone else might tell her, and make me look like I was holding out on important things regarding our relationship.

"I hope you don't fall in love with her," Ariel said, beginning to sob. I was foolish for telling her so soon, I realized, especially when she was still in a very vulnerable state.

"But I don't love her.... I never did....I was just confused. I love only you. How could I not love you when you were willing to quit smoking for me?" It seemed strange to me that I hadn't noticed her going without cigarettes for the past few days.

"You were talking to the staff about me! I told them not to tell you I was quitting smoking! It was probably Tina who told you!" Tears flowed down Ariel's face as she turned and ran down the hall. I felt like kicking my butt with the power of a donkey. How could I have been so insensitive? I was going to run after Ariel, but suddenly Angela and another nurse were there, telling me to give her space because she had just gotten out of seclusion.

"Come with me, Don, and I'll get you a PRN of Ativan. Dr. Hilton has ordered it for agitation. You'll feel better, and it'll help ease your mind about Ariel," soothed Angela.

"Whatever," I said, totally dejected. I walked like a robot with them to the nurses' office. I took the Ativan handed to me. Angela then told me to get some rest, and she would see me in a little while. I knew she had to go check up on Ariel, who was also her patient, so I agreed. I hoped Angela could get Ariel to understand my position and my feelings towards Ariel. I went into my room to rest. I laid on my bed, thinking of Ariel's rollercoaster emotions, until I settled into a light sleep.

I awoke with Angela standing over me and telling me it was dinnertime. She told me I had slept for two hours. I said that I felt better. Then I asked her how Ariel was doing. She said that Ariel was okay, but she also said that she wasn't allowed to discuss Ariel's illness with another patient. I told her I understood because I wouldn't want the confidentiality of my records and history revealed to people who were not staff.

I rose from my bed and followed Angela down the depressing white halls and into the gloomy dayroom. It had started to rain while I was asleep which, with my illness, made the window view almost completely demonic. I recalled the song by The Doors, "People Are Strange," where Jim Morrison sang "faces come out of the rain / when you're strange." I sensed a touch to my elbow, which brought

## The Temptress Ariel

me back to the now dependant dayroom. It was Angela, asking me if I was all right.

"Yeah, I'm okay, just a little down because I miss Ariel," I sighed as I found my dinner tray. I looked around and saw Ariel sitting with her back to me across the large dayroom as she ate her supper and talked to another woman seated next to her.

"Sit here, Don," Angela said, motioning to a seat beside Dale. "Dale, Don is going to join you for dinner. Maybe you can get to know each other a little more."

I knew that the staff had observed me talking to Dale earlier because the TV room, the dayroom, and the exit door in the hall were under surveillance. I had seen the TV screens in the office. I was still a bit afraid that my room had a camera, although I hadn't found one there. I felt Angela's hand on my shoulder as she told me to sit down.

"I'm sorry, Angela," I said. "It's just that I've got a lot on my mind."

"Oh, Don, you don't have to explain. I understand."

"Thanks, Angela," I said as I nodded to Dale.

"I'm off in an hour, so don't forget to check the board by the office to see who your designated nurse is; also, it will tell you your level or status. Don, I think—I'm not sure—but I think you get your clothes back. So you're moving up a level. Just try to relax and continue to get better. I'll be back tomorrow. Feel free to approach staff with your problems or concerns. Enjoy your dinner," Angela said, walking away.

My dinner consisted of mashed potatoes with gravy, roast beef, peas, and carrots. My tray also had milk and apple pie. The food was surprisingly good, considering it was hospital food. I asked Dale to pass the salt but he seemed lost in thought as he ate. I gently touched his arm, and he was startled.

"I didn't mean to bother you, Dale, but could you please pass the salt?" I was a little apprehensive regarding his reaction. But he whispered "sorry" and gave me the salt. I felt selfish that I had thought Angela wanted Dale to provide support and friendship for me, when in fact Dale needed more help than me. I thanked him, and I asked him if he'd like to play cards later. However, he just sat looking at his dinner, and shook his head no.

I finished my dinner but dallied with my milk, because I was hoping to time my tray return with Ariel's. I could only see the back of her canary-yellow housecoat; her hair flowed into a ponytail. Finally she rose, still talking to the rather attractive woman who was rising too. But I was starting to shake, I was so frightened that Ariel might not like me anymore. I accidentally dropped my dinner tray, which caused most of the patients to jump a little. Then, Angela was helping me pick up the things I had dropped, when suddenly I felt a gentle, arousing touch on my back: I turned to see that it was Ariel's hand, and she smiled that champion of smiles. I was more in love with Ariel than ever.

"Are you, okay, Don?" asked Ariel as she helped me and Angela with my tray.

"Yeah, I'm fine. How about yourself?" I asked, trying to control my somewhat shaky voice. We put our trays back.

"I'm better, and I'm sorry." Angela looked at Ariel and me, and told us to go for meds as she left the room. "I know you love me, Don. If you didn't, you wouldn't have followed me here, you would have stayed with Tina. And when I touched you on the back you trembled. I know that you sensed it was me. Maybe it was karma. I love you!"

"I love you too, hon. Honest. Only you," I mushed. But, this small-talk was a big turn-on for us. I kissed her on a slightly flushed cheek, and then we dawdled as we walked the hall to the med room. We got in line, and I told her I might be getting my clothes back soon.

"Oh, Don, that would be great if we both got our clothes back and then climbed another level so we could go on short outings with staff. It beats being locked up here."

"Yeah, that would be nice, but anywhere that I'm with you is great. Just listen to the nurses and doctors and we'll be outta here in no time," I said enthusiastically. "Together."

"You don't have to tell me who to listen to. I know the ropes, probably more than you do. But," Ariel's tone softened, "I would like for us to get out together. Then, we could have some privacy." She smiled coyly, tilting her head and holding out a hand for meds. She downed them, and winked at me as she turned away. I was frightened that she wasn't taking her meds; then I remembered she had said she always took meds in hospitals. I took my meds, and was about to follow Ariel down the hall when a nurse handed me my clothes.

"We're going to check that your clothes and things are all in order," said the nurse. "Oh, by the way, Don, my name is Maria. I will be your evening nurse." I didn't like her approach too much, especially when she said my name without ever having been introduced to me. But I went with her into my room where she placed my clothes on the bed. She also gave me my ring and watch. I checked my wallet, and told her that everything was there, including my ID and forty-two dollars cash.

She told me to get dressed as she left my room. She seemed a little bossy, more so than the daynurse, Angela, even.

I decided to shower first, which I knew would impress the nurses and get them to loosen my leash a little, allowing Ariel and I to play kissy-face and love-starved bunny-rabbits. I grabbed a clean towel in my bathroom and went to the office, looking for help. Maria was pleased that I had taken the initiative to groom myself, so she gave me some shampoo and some soap and a face-cloth. I walked down the hallway and realized that I was probably cleaning myself more for Ariel than for any other reason. This thought brought an inadvertent smile to my face which I quickly erased because of the paranoia and tension in the ward. I didn't want to make waves, except with Ariel, I joked to myself.

I was soon in an unlocked shower room, and before long I was lathering with soap and shampoo; the hot shower felt great. I closed my eyes and began to dream of Ariel, seeing her picturesque smile and feeling the warmth and softness of her kiss. I began to fantasize about us living together in our own house, with our own children, and having a normal family life. I would be working, and so would Ariel if she wanted to. I began to whistle and sing Sister Sledge's song "We Are Family," although I could barely hear myself since the shower was loud.

After I shampooed for a second time, I rinsed and then turned off the shower. I reached for my towel, but it wasn't where I had placed it. I started to think that I'd dropped it on the floor, but suddenly my towel was in strange hands, rubbing my head. I turned to see who was there.

# Chapter 9

I turned to see Ariel holding a towel. We were both naked and then embracing and kissing in the steamy shower. My mouth tasted her neck and breasts; my tongue moved over her body like a cat's.
Our hands explored each other until we were flying high with passion on the floor making love.

We were pulled apart by Maria and several other nurses.

"Get dressed, Don. And don't do this here again. Ariel, we're going to put you in seclusion for this. You don't—I repeat don't—follow men into the showers! Get your pyjamas on," said an angry Maria.

"It was my fault, Maria," I said. "I wanted Ariel in here." Which was the truth, although I hadn't planned it. Ariel beamed me a brief smile.

"Nice try, Don. But we saw Ariel come in after you," retorted Maria.

We got dressed and I pleaded Ariel's case once again as the security guards took Ariel away. But the staff told me they knew what had happened and reminded me that I was in a hospital to get well again. They also said that having unprotected sex was dangerous, and that mental patients seldom considered the results of their actions. Maria frowned and told me Ariel and I had done a very foolish thing.

I got to my room and finished dressing. Then, I paced the halls like a caged cat by the seclusion rooms, but I saw no sign of Ariel. I was getting worried; I hoped she was okay. Maybe she was sleeping. Perhaps they had given her more medication to relax her. Finally, a nurse came out of the windowed office and asked me if I needed a PRN. I said no, but realized it was her way of telling me to move on away from the seclusion rooms. She knew I was obsessed with Ariel's situation.

I told the nurse I was going for tea; she responded with a nod and a smile. I walked past several people and said hello to them as I entered into the day room. Dale was seated at a table playing cards with Maria. I said hi and put the kettle on. The dayroom was brightly lit, which helped inch up my mood. Then Maria turned to me and asked me if I would like to go to the Chapel service in the hospital in twenty minutes. It was outside the ward but on the same floor. So far only Dale and she were going, she told me.

"I'd like to go, as long as they don't start preaching hellfire and other crap like that," I said, and surprised myself with my anger.

"Oh, no, Don. It's not like that. It's a very positive, relaxed little service. And if it gets to be too much for you or Dale we can always leave."

"Okay, I'll go. It'll be a nice change from this ward," I said. Maria's doe brown eyes gleamed with satisfaction. I made my tea and sat down, watching them play casino. I wasn't surprised that Dale won, because I could see Maria's hand and her deliberately poor plays. I finished my tea and went to my room, lost in thought about Ariel and the service. I had been to church before, and had often found the people there to be judgmental and fault-seeking. I only wanted to be with Ariel forever, I thought, as I sat on the edge of my bed, looking out at the bright city lights of Surrey, Vancouver's largest suburb.

"Are you, okay, Don?" I was slightly startled, and turned to see Maria and Dale standing next to me.

"Oh, yeah, I'm okay, Maria. I was just thinking about Ariel. Are we going to the service now?" I recovered.

"Yes."

The three of us then left the ward, passed security, and turned right down a hallway. As we approached the chapel, Maria reminded us that if it got to be too much for us, to tell her. She wasn't a mind reader,

## The Temptress Ariel

she told us. After we entered the chapel, Maria told us to sit in a back pew, and looking deep into our faces she said she would sit between us.

There were about a dozen or so people at the service, and it was not long before a preacher got up to speak. He smiled and began by welcoming people of all faiths. This helped relax me a little, and I was pleasantly surprised when the sermon went smoothly. When it came time to pray, I prayed that Ariel and I would live together forever. But only to myself.

As we rose to leave, the preacher shook our hands and thanked us for coming. I asked him if he would pray for my girlfriend's health, and I was a bit surprised when he smiled and said that he would.

The three of us walked back to the ward, calmly discussing how smoothly the service had gone. Maria told the other nurses that Dale and I had presented ourselves with much maturity, when we got back. I made a quick round of the halls and saw Ariel's face in the seclusion window.

"Don! It's Ariel! Help me! Let me out!"

"I can't, Ariel. I'm sorry," I said, almost in tears. Then, I saw the girl who had thought I was Luke Skywalker approach me, eating black licorice.

"Hi, Luke! It's Princess Leia!" she said.

"Please don't call me that. My name is Don," I said assertively.

"Would you like something to eat?" she replied. "How about these?" She then lifted her top, revealing her bare breasts. I heard Ariel scream at her, and a nurse named Elaine was suddenly beside me.

"Nancy, we're going to put you in the quiet room for that. Are you okay, Don?" Elaine asked, as two security guards stood by.

"Yes, and it would take a lot more than that to get a rise out of me," I said as Nancy winced, and was taken away. I could hear Ariel laughing, just then.

I smiled at her, but Elaine told me it was snack time in the dayroom, and to stay away from the seclusion rooms. I agreed and proceeded down the hall.

I saw Dale making tea in the dayroom, and asked him if I could have some. He nodded and then introduced me to an older man named Tommy, who was an Englishman. He was friendly like Dale, and he told me that I didn't seem psychotic, so I'd probably get out soon, possibly in a day or two. I thanked him and the three of us settled down at a table with our tea; we also helped ourselves to the cookies and apples provided for snacktime.

Tommy told us stories about the sixties in England, and how he'd met John Lennon and Peter Townshend. When I told him The Who was my favorite band, he said that he had taught Townshend how to play the guitar. I knew he was delusional, but I just smiled.

"Why are you here, Tommy?" I asked. "Did the rock'n'roll lifestyle get to you?"

"I'm here because I need to smoke marijuana and they won't let me. I need it to be healthy. But, no, they stick a needle up my bum every week. I gave up the rock scene when the government began using me for military experiments. They've given me almost every drug except pot– the only one I really need. I am a prisoner here, I am."

I noticed Dale seemed a little quiet and withdrawn, which reminded me of his low mood this morning. I was pretty certain that he was manic-depressive, due to his mood swings. I asked Dale how he was feeling.

"I don't want to bring anybody else down by talking about my depression," he said, which answered my question. Just then, a big biker-type man whom I had seen at dinner came in the dayroom and sat down by Dale.

"Ya look like hell, Dale. Still down with those nightmares? That's the shits," he said gruffly. Dale introduced Tommy and me to him. His name was Jay.

"We lived in the same boarding home for two years, me and Jay," Dale explained.

I pictured Jay's long, brown hair flying as he rode a motorcycle.

"What are you here for, Don? You seem a little more stable than most of the people here. Are you gonna be let out soon?" Jay asked.

"I had a mild relapse when my girlfriend got sick. Many years ago I got sick when my Mom died because I couldn't cope without her. And I used to do a lot of LSD in my teens. But I'm on good meds now, and I'm waiting for my girlfriend Ariel to get better– she's in seclusion right now on this ward."

"You didn't say Ariel, did you? Short, long black hair, kind of cute?"

"Yeah, that's her. How do you know her?" I asked, slightly alarmed.

"I know her ex-boyfriend, Stan. He's a real fucking asshole: he treated her like shit, as he does everybody. I'd keep her and yourself away from him. But if he hassles you two, let me know and I'll kick his ass. You're a friend of Dale's and you've got your shit together. That's good enough for me." Jay turned to Tommy and asked him his reason for being here.

"When the marines landed in Surrey, they captured me and took me to the war criminal, Dr. Hilton. He experiments with drugs in this hospital. We're all guinea pigs," Tommy said. "If they would just let me smoke pot, I would be fine." Jay said he understood where Tommy was coming from in a way, because he, too, liked pot.

We continued talking until a very ill woman barged into the dayroom, saying her name was Ruth. Her eyes bulged and her enormous stomach jiggled.

"God will judge and send you people to hell if you smoke cigarettes or drink alcohol. I hope you people don't smoke! I'm a Christian and I have to tell people not to sin. I don't sin. In fact, I'm pregnant with Jesus. Someday, he will be born once more and rule the world. So you'd better be good," Ruth spieled.

Elaine and Maria came in and told Ruth to stop bothering others. Ruth turned and stomped out of the room. We could hear her open the smoking room door and begin talking.

"Stop gossipping about me! I'm a good person! I'm a Christian!" she said, and left before the nurses caught up to her.

"I guess now we're Ruthless," joked Jay, and we all laughed at the old joke.

After awhile, meds were called and we went and got in line by the nurses' station. I was surprised to see Ariel at the front of the line; when she turned after getting her meds she saw Jay and beamed at him.

"Jay, it's so good to see you! How are you doing?" asked a somewhat surprised Ariel. "Have you seen Stan lately?"

"I'm fine. Yeah, Stan's living in a boarding home a couple of blocks from here. Chauncey House." Then, Ariel saw me at the back of the line, and she blanched and paled like a frightened ghost.

I was angry, and looked away as she approached me.

"Hi, Don," she said timidly. "I hope you aren't upset because I was asking about Stan. I was just curious."

"If you're not willing to forget about him, then why bother with me? I'm tired of always hearing about him. But I do love you, Ariel." It hurt us both for me to say these things but inside I was adamant. I refused to hear about Stan.

"I'm sorry, Don," she said with tears in her eyes. This melted my heart a bit.

"It's okay. But from now on our love is just you and me. Right?" I felt a surge of happiness run through me when she nodded and neoned me that smile that I loved.

"I'm going to bed now, Don. They gave me Halcion which makes you sleep. But we'll be together tomorrow, I hope," she said wistfully, like a little girl.

I was aching to kiss her goodnight but I held back, and just said goodnight instead.

"Are you two quite finished?" asked Maria, the nurse; I realized I was the last patient to get meds. As Maria handed my meds to me, I watched Ariel walk down the hallway into her room.

"How are you feeling tonight, Don?" Maria interrupted.

"Oh, a little down but not too bad, I guess. I think I'll watch a little TV to feel more on an even keel."

"That's a very good idea," Maria responded, very pleased. "Don't forget though, bed-time is at ten. So you've got less than an hour to watch TV."

I proceeded to the TV room and I found Jay watching "Cheers," a show I liked. I sat down beside him just as a commercial came on.

"Jay, I was wondering if you could tell me something about this Stan guy who Ariel was engaged to."

"Sure. He looks a lot like you. Slightly overweight — no offence — medium height, blonde-colored hair, only his is a bit longer at the back. You both sound the same when you talk. When I first saw you here I noticed you looked like Stan But he just used Ariel. Every once in a while, though, she tries to get back with him. I hope she stays with you, 'cause you seem peaceful. Stan is always in trouble, it seems."

"What types of trouble does he get into?"

"Mostly theft. Steer clear of him."

The show came back on, and I watched the remainder of it with Jay. When it ended, we both yawned.

"Well, I don't know about you, Don, but I'm gonna hit the hay. I'm exhausted. This Olanzapine really makes you tired."

"I'm on Olanzapine too, and I've noticed it helps me sleep better also. See ya tomorrow, Jay."

"See ya, Don." I walked to my room slowly, thinking of the potential problems involving Ariel, me, and Stan. I went and got undressed and climbed into bed. I felt drowsy and drifted into a dream.

## ❃❱ Chapter 10 ❰❃

Ariel and I were horseback riding. Her horse, Teddy, was almost flying down by the sea where the red eye of morning, the sun, was rising. I was thrilled beyond belief when Pegasus, my horse, passed Ariel and began to fly with me over the sea. We rode high above the eagles in the sky. I turned to see Teddy stumble far beneath us and Ariel fall into the wheatfield. I shouted Ariel's name and turned my winged horse back towards the ground.

We seemed to be moving in slow-motion as we approached the earth. Finally, we reached the ground just as Ariel's face turned up at me. I cried out "No, No, No!" when her face turned into a skull-and-crossbones. Then Teddy rose into the air and raced away, at the same time whinnying with delight at being rid of Ariel.

I awoke and felt a hand shaking my shoulder gently, saying it was okay, that I had just been dreaming. I didn't recognize the nurse but I asked her where Ariel was immediately. She said her name was Amy and that Ariel was fine.

I told her about my dream and that I was afraid something bad was going to happen to Ariel. I felt bad karma, I told her, but Amy just said the nightmare was making me a bit ill, and that it was understandable for me to react with fear and apprehension. Also, she told me that Ariel was safe here and getting the best of care in the province. After these words I began to calm down. Amy left saying I should try to sleep, and that if I needed extra medication, Dr. Hilton had prescribed a milligram of Ativan for my PRN. I thanked her but told her I was calmer now and would try to sleep. She patted my head and left.

I awoke with a start when I heard Amy's soft voice saying it was time for meds. She told me she was leaving now and that Angela would be my day nurse; she was waiting to give me meds. I looked at my watch and saw it was 8:00 a.m. Amy asked me how I'd slept after the nightmare. I said fine. She exited the room so I could get dressed. I then went and got my meds.

"And how are you today?" asked a very friendly Angela.

"I'm okay. I just had a bad dream," I answered as I swallowed my pills with a cup of orange juice.

"Would you like to see Dr. Hilton today?"

"Why? Am I being discharged?" I asked hopefully. Then I thought about Ariel and how I wanted to be near her.

"Are you listening to me, Don?" Angela asked firmly.

"Yeah...um...I was wondering if I was being discharged."

"And I told you Dr. Hilton said it was too soon. Do you still want to see him?"

"Not today. Maybe tomorrow. My meds are okay right now, anyhow."

"How about if I put you down to see Dr. Hilton tomorrow morning at 9 a.m.?"

"That's fine." It really wasn't because I didn't want a med change. Plus, I knew that the nurses recorded and reported all the patients' behavior for the doctors.

"Good," said Angela.

I felt a little sick to my stomach as I walked down to the dayroom for breakfast. I was the last one to eat, and much to my chagrin, Ariel was not in the room. I got my tray and sat down beside Tommy, the Englishman, who was finishing his morning tea.

"Hello, Don, my mate. How'd you sleep?"

"Oh, so-so. I had a nightmare about Ariel, but I'm over it now." I began to eat my breakfast.

"Well, try and relax. And whatever you do, don't let Dr. Hilton experiment with new drugs on you. He's a tricky one, he is." I thanked Tommy but didn't really believe him. Many doctors had helped me.

## The Temptress Ariel

Tommy patted me on the back after he got up to leave and said that he was going to lie down. I told him that I'd talk to him later.

I finished my breakfast while I was thinking of Ariel and how I wanted to spend time with my little dear. I was beginning to wonder if I was getting somewhat mushy with all the pet names, yet my own mushy endearments made me love her more.

I was going to look for Ariel, but I decided to wait because I felt tired. I resolved to take a nap. I left the dayroom and almost bumped into Nancy.

"Have you seen Hans Solo, Luke?" she asked me.

"No. And please stop calling me Luke."

"Whatever!" she said and left in a huff.

I heard a familiar giggle, and I turned to see Ariel by the smoking room door watching me with amusement.

"That's telling her, Don!" she laughed.

I was surprised to see her with jeans and a sweater on.

"When did you get your clothes back, hon?" I blurted before I realized what a dumb question it was.

"After I saw Dr. Hilton this morning. He said I was getting better. But you look tired, Don. Maybe you should rest and we'll talk later. Besides, I'm going for a cigarette. Is that okay with you?" Her eyes searched mine as she spoke.

"By all means go ahead, Ariel. We'll rap later. Thanks for being so understanding." I returned to my room and slid onto my bed. The next thing I knew, Angela was waking me for lunch. I got up, still sleepy, and said I'd be there for lunch in a minute. I went into the washroom and doused my face with cold water. It felt good. I looked in the mirror and noticed that I had bags under my eyes. Probably from worrying about Ariel, I thought.

I entered the dayroom and saw Ariel wave at me. I got my lunch tray and joined her at a table where she was eating alone.

"Hi, hon," I said as I sat down next to her. I was becoming turned on by the smell of her hair and perfume and by how physically close together we were. Suddenly, we were joined by Dale and Jay who Ariel already knew.

"How's it going guys?" I asked, although I was hoping to be alone with Ariel.

"Better," said Dale.

"I'm fine," added Jay.

We started talking about the food, and how it was fairly good here. Ariel and I gave our rice pudding to Jay, who said that it was his favorite desert.

"I'm trying to lose weight," explained Ariel, and I echoed that I was trying to lose weight too. Dale didn't want either of our rice puddings because he was not that hungry. But Jay gobbled them down, slopping some on his goatee.

"Don, you never did tell us your diagnosis or very much about your past," stated Jay between spoonfuls of pudding.

"I have a minor case of Schizophrenia," I replied.

"Paranoid Schizophrenia?" Jay asked.

"No. I'm not paranoid, and I wish everybody would quit thinking that I am." The four of us laughed at my joke.

"You sound like some of Dale's wit has rubbed off on you," Jay grinned.

"Unfortunately, only half of it," I jested, and we all chuckled at this variation on the old joke. "But seriously, I began to use pot and LSD when my parents divorced. I flipped out on LSD one night when I came home to my mom's empty old house. Until then, I was for acid–acid wasn't a bad place to be crazy when my mom would be at her boyfriend's for weeks at a time. Which meant I had to scrounge for food and cigarette money. When I flipped out on acid, I swore I would never do it again. It traumatized me.

"But you know, they wouldn't have been so bad, those lonely nights, if I knew how to make friends, especially girlfriends. I usually had one good friend all the years I was growing up, but it wasn't until my mom died...um...when I was at UBC that I began to deteriorate into psychosis. And my first...uh...girlfriend...uh... Sylvia....cheated on me with my only friend, Ron. When I wouldn't forgive her she committed suicide, just after my mother had died. They were close." Tears began streaking down my face, but I had a story to tell as fast as I could.

"Finally, after I got into a fistfight on a bus I was sent to hospital. A few months later I moved into a psychiatric boarding home. I became very close to a nurse named Jane who, like Sylvia, committed suicide.

"So, I tried to commit suicide...." I said, my lips quivering. "That's when.....I.... started...... hearing voices of demons .... I always believed in a God, but I don't believe in hellfire and all that crap. I believe what the master poet John Milton said: 'The mind is its own place, and in itself can make a Heav'n of Hell, a Hell of Heav'n.'

"I'm sorry if I brought you guys down with all this negative shit, but I believe in love and goodness as opposed to all the violence and terror the Bible documents and has been used for. How's that for a spiel?"

"Don, you never told me Sylvia committed suicide. Why not?" Ariel asked, her eyes looking down on her lunch tray.

"I didn't want to upset you, hon. You had just moved into Solgate and I didn't want to lay my guilt on you so soon." I reached towards her and gently pulled her chin up. "I love you, Ariel." Then, I turned to Dale and Jay.

"I hope I didn't depress you guys. I guess it's time for meds," I said, deliberately changing the subject. Dale and Jay said my story was interesting as the four of us put our trays on the racks. We went and got our meds.

Ariel asked me if I'd like to join her in the smoking room while she had her cigarette. I said that I'd rather not because it was too smoky in there. She looked a little hurt, so I changed my mind and said I'd go there with her.

"I don't want you doing it because you feel forced to," she said, her eyes glistening. "I guess I'll see you later."

I tried to kiss her on the cheek, but she turned away and went into the smoking room. I went into my room and slid onto my bed, face down on my pillow. I was afraid I'd spilled the beans too much on Ariel with my depressing life, and that not giving in to her request for me to join her in the smoking room may have tipped the barrel. I was scared and began to cry. Soon after, I fell asleep.

Angela woke me, saying I had slept most of the day away. It was nearly dinnertime, so she told me to wash up and get ready. She asked me if my medication was too sedating. If it was, she told me, we could bring it up with Dr. Hilton tomorrow. I said it was okay. She told me if I needed to talk, she was available. Suddenly, I found myself unburdening my mind with how I had dumped my history onto the shoulders of Ariel, Dale, and Jay.

"Don, if they asked you, then it's their duty to deal with it. You're not responsible for how they feel."

"But Ariel didn't ask. And now she's not speaking to me."

"Oh, I'm sure she'll come around. She's not the type to hold a grudge. Don't worry, just get ready for dinner. Okay?" Angela left my room.

I went down the white-walled hallway after washing up, dreading facing Ariel. I was surprised to see that Ariel had finished eating, and was just leaving the dayroom. But, when she flashed that winning smile and winked at me, my heart melted my face into a grin. I sat down beside Jay and asked him if he wanted my blueberry pie. Before I could tell him it was because I wanted to lose weight for Ariel, he had it off my plate.

"You don't like blueberry pie, do ya?" he asked.

"No, I do like it. It's just that I'm trying to cut down on my sugar. I'm going to drop a few pounds for Ariel."

"You shouldn't worry about things like that. She loves ya, man. And that would mean she's shallow if she changes her mind. So then she wouldn't be worth having in the first place, if she thinks like that."

"Thanks, Jay," I said.

We finished our meals in silence. Then we went for meds. I was hoping to see Ariel; I was afraid that she might be back in seclusion, since I hadn't seen her at meds.

I began pacing the rectangular route around the halls, conscious that I had more energy. I went by the smoking room, glancing through the small window to see if Ariel was in there. She wasn't. I went past the nurses' station and on into the TV room. Tommy was watching some English program. I nodded to him, then turned back to my pacing. I went past the nurses again and felt their scrutiny. Down the south side of the hall were the women's rooms; I walked by them, not knowing which was Ariel's room.

I hesitated slightly as I passed a room because I could hear Eleanor's stern voice. Then, when I heard Ariel, I breathed a sigh of relief and went to the dayroom; I was glad she wasn't in seclusion.

I saw Dale making tea and I asked him if I could have some too. He grinned and said yes.

"Where are you from, Dale?" I asked as he poured the tea. We went to a table with our cups.

"Originally, Winnipeg. But my family moved here when I was ten. I had a nervous breakdown when I was sixteen. It's been a long uphill battle ever since. I was in Riverview, the provincial hospital, for four years. But I'm much better now. My parents are divorced, but my mom still comes to visit me."

"That's rough," I said. "I didn't break down until I was twenty-one. And I know I'm lucky that I was never sent to Riverview."

"Speaking of Riverview, I guess you heard that they sent Ruth there today. She was totally psychotic."

"No, I hadn't heard. I slept all afternoon."

"Yeah, well it was probably just as well; she was in bad shape. Plus you seem more rested now."

"Yeah, I am."

"Are you going to the chapel service tonight?" Dale asked.

"Oh. I'd forgotten about that. Yeah, I'd like to go When is it?"

"In about an hour with Maria."

"Great! This ward can be so depressing--not the people, just the...you know....despondent atmosphere."

"I know only too well, unfortunately."

"Are there any women here that you like? Maybe being in love could help ease your depression. I'm not talking about just sex: being sex-starved is unfortunate; being love-starved is tragic. I found that out with Ariel. She means everything to me. My whole world revolves around her, and while she can be a little shit occasionally, she's...uh....so sweet and charming and gorgeous that I can't stand being away from her. Hell, I'm starting to sound like someone out of a soap opera or a Harlequin romance. But I don't care– I love her."

"I can see your thought processes are running wild about her. You asked me a question, then spieled on about Ariel. I understand; I do it myself. Just so you know. But I'm not looking for a girlfriend right now. I will when I feel ready."

"Fair enough. And thanks for the feedback. Maybe I was spouting off like a whale."

We finished our tea, talking about The Grizzlies and The Canucks, two of Vancouver's pro sports teams. I was quite surprised that he knew more about them than I did. We really hit it off when we both said that Shareef of The Grizzlies was our favorite player.

Maria came into the dayroom as we were about to leave and said the chapel service would begin in half an hour. We both let her know we were going, and I told her I needed to get cleaned up. This pleased her, since nurses like it when patients take positive initiatives. So, I groomed myself, rested for about ten minutes, and then I went to the nurses' station and was delighted to see Ariel there.

"Hi, Ariel!" I said happily. "Are you going to the service with us?"

"Yes, Don," said Ariel coyly. "I missed us last night." She was wearing a white Angora sweater with blue jeans; her hair was done up in a bun with a few strands dangling down each side of her face.

"Well, once we're out of here we'll go together all the time, I hope. How is your grandma, by the way?"

"She's the same. She visited me today. She brought me a carton of smokes. I hope you don't mind me smoking, Don."

"You don't need to smoke, because you're already hot." Even Dale and Maria laughed at what I said. "Seriously I don't mind. Because I used to smoke myself, so I understand."

"Aren't you warm in that jacket, Dale?" Maria asked suddenly.

He said that he was and took it off, revealing a Grizzlies T-shirt. I was wearing a B.C. Lions sweater and I joked that Vancouver's sports teams would be well represented before The Lord tonight. I noticed Dale was wearing glasses; I hadn't seen him wearing them before. Maybe he used contacts as well. But I didn't ask him if he did. He was looking a little down again.

"Are we ready to go?" asked Maria, who was a vision of grey beauty: she wore a grey turtle-neck sweater, a long grey skirt, and matching boots.

Ariel nudged me, giving me a hurt look; I realized I had been staring at Maria. But there was no way I would ever give up Ariel. Not even for ten Marias. I grinned at this thought, because I couldn't comprehend going out with more than one woman. Ariel alone was too much for me.

"What's going on, Don?" asked Maria. "Do you feel okay?"

" Never better," I recovered. "I'm just happy because Ariel is joining us tonight."

"Well, try to concentrate on the service, all right?" Maria said gently. I knew she didn't appreciate me sizing her up. But it was unintentional.

"Sure, but remember we're only human," I said, because I noticed Dale had given Maria a good looking over. So we began the walk down the hall, through the only exit doors of the ward, past security, and entered into the little chapel. I looked at my watch as we sat in a back pew. It was 7 p.m.

I was glad that I got to sit beside Ariel. Aroused by her perfume and soft warmth, I sat extra close. Then, the service began, and the Bible-thumping preacher gave his sermon, although I couldn't concentrate on it because Ariel had slipped her hand into mine. Every minute or so we would look deep in each other's eyes and smile with love. It felt right, too. For weren't temples and churches created for love?

All too soon the service was over and the two dozen or so people, including us, left the chapel after shaking hands with the minister. It didn't surprise me that Ariel and I were the only ones he said nothing to. Not even a thank you. But I was happy as a lark. Ariel and I held hands all the way back to the ward. When we got there Dale said he was tired and needed to rest.

Maria looked at me and Ariel as she made her report to the head or charge nurse that we had behaved well at the chapel. She told us it was snacktime; Ariel and I walked down the hallway holding hands. Nancy came out of the dayroom holding a half-eaten peanut-butter sandwich just as we were going in.

"Hi, Luke! I see you've found your lover. But what about me? As Princess Leia I need to find Hans Solo. Can you help me?" she asked, as Ariel glared at her. I was afraid of a scene, but fortunately a nurse behind us spoke to her.

"Nancy, stop bothering people." At these words, Nancy walked on past us.

"Bitch," I heard Ariel mutter softly.

"Ariel, she's sick," I whispered. We went into the dayroom and we each ate a peanut-butter sandwich and had a cup of tea. When I asked her what seclusion was like, she became very quiet and said it was scary. I quickly changed the subject by saying we'd probably be back in Solgate within a few days. She looked up at me with a doleful expression in her gorgeous eyes and I gave her a kiss on the lips to cheer her up. It only helped a little, it seemed. Then, Maria came and sat next to us and asked us if we'd like to play cards.

"No, I want to watch some TV," said Ariel.

"I do, too," I said, desperate to be with Ariel. Maria said that would be fine. She was glad we were keeping occupied, but suggested we socialize with other patients also.

We left the dayroom hand-in-hand, and some of the patients pacing the halls stopped to stare. I realized I hadn't met many of the twenty-five or thirty other patients here. We reached the TV room and I was overjoyed to find it empty. Ariel was glad, too.

We began watching "Frasier," a show I hadn't seen much, but one that Ariel liked. At every commercial we kissed even though there was a camera in the room. Surprisingly, no one else came into the room until the TV show was over. Maria then peeked into the room, telling us it was med-time. We followed her down to the line up for meds.

After getting our meds, Ariel said she was tired and that she would see me in the morning.

"Halcion makes me very sleepy," she yawned.

"Well, I'll walk you to your room."

"Thank-you." Ariel smiled, making me want to cover her with as many kisses as a leopard has spots. We again walked down the hallway holding hands as people watched. Then, in front of her room's door, I kissed her for at least a full minute.

"You two can come up for air now!" I heard Maria say behind me.

"I was just giving her a kiss goodnight," I said, slightly pissed off at Maria for treating us like children.

"Well, make it snappy. Some of the older patients have complained about you two. There is no love-making here. You're here to get well, not– "

"To have fun?" I interrupted.

"You know what I mean, Don. And you too, Ariel. Try to show some restraint."

"Goodnight, Don," said Ariel, her eyelashes fluttering, her mouth playfully open.

"Goodnight, Ariel," I grinned. Then, turning to Maria, I said, "I hope this will be acceptable for the Furher."

"Don't be smart, Don," Maria frowned.

"Words to live by in here," I said, and Ariel went into her room laughing.

"Don, if you can't control yourself, we'll put you in the quiet room."

"All right," I answered begrudgingly. I turned and went into the dayroom, where I poured myself a cup of tea. I saw Dale and went to sit beside him, but he got up and left without saying a word. He seemed very depressed. I hoped I hadn't upset him by my behavior with Ariel. Then I thought to myself that I felt good about my time with Ariel and no one had the right to judge us. After all, love was what life was all about.

I sat down in the empty dayroom and I drank my tea. A nurse named Bea, who was tall and very bubbly, came in the room and asked me how I was feeling. I said that I felt relaxed and in the mood to write a poem. She nearly ran faster than Donovan Bailey getting me a pencil and some paper from a locked cupboard. Creativity was always encouraged but not enforced here, unlike many other hospitals. I gratefully accepted the pen and paper and I began to write a poem about Ariel. After about twenty minutes I'd completed the first draft.

I read the poem to Bea. "It's called 'Ariel,' " I said. "By Don Waters."

> Ariel, through life's dark tunnel we go
> But like a stream of light our love will flow
> One day we'll roam in Elysian flowers
> Where skies shine more brilliant and beyond ours
> Ariel, your smile will be the light's heart
> Ariel, from those fields we'll never part
> We will live in shining enlightenment
> I can't say how precious our love has meant
> This poem has words that I plan to live by
> Together we'll live, Ariel and I.

I knew it wasn't a particularly good poem because my meter was rusty and the poem itself was almost as sentimental as a Hallmark card. But Bea liked it and said that it showed strong, positive feelings. I thanked her and took it back to my room. I put it on my brown night table beneath the lamp. I read the poem once more. It had an eerie effect on me. But maybe I was just tired. I climbed into bed and began dreaming of Ariel.

## Chapter 11

Ariel rode Teddy, her horse, down by the sea. The red eye of morning rose like a foaming cauldron as Pegasus, my horse, passed Ariel and Teddy. Pegasus began to fly like a plane taking off, and I looked down to see Ariel fall off Teddy as he stumbled in a wheatfield.

I shouted Ariel's name as Pegasus turned around and started to dive past the eagles towards the ground where Ariel had fallen.

I reached Ariel after what seemed like an eternity, and she turned her face up at me. I cried out "No! No! No!" after her face turned into a skull-and-crossbones. Then Teddy rose with a maniacal neighing, which I knew meant he had killed her. I screamed, "Ariel!"

Suddenly, I felt a jostling of my shoulder and I woke up facing Amy, the night nurse.

"It's okay, Don. You just had a bad dream," soothed Amy. I told her that it was almost exactly the same as the nightmare I had had last night. I said recurring dreams and bad symbols and events meant bad karma; I was worried sick about Ariel because of them, I told Amy.

"Don, your dreams are yours. So how can they affect Ariel? This is a type of thought projection."

"No, it isn't. Something bad is going to happen."

"Don, I will get you a PRN of Ativan to help calm you down and help you sleep more peacefully. I'll be right back." Amy left, her long black hair flowing down her back the way Ariel's did, I thought.

I was terrified as a trapped mouse; I realized I was sweating even though it was cool in my room. I prayed to the gods to help keep Ariel safe.

"Here we go!" said Amy as she came in my room with a med cup.

"Take this, Don. You'll feel much better. Try and sleep, and if you can't or you need to talk just come to the office. But please don't worry about Ariel. You have to take care of yourself first. All right?"

"Okay," I said, slightly shaky. "I think I'll be able to sleep better now. I guess I should tell Dr. Hilton about these dreams," I mused rather uncertainly.

"Don, that is a very good idea and a positive sign. It shows that you are thinking ahead and that your nightmares are signs of the stress that we all have. I'm glad you're gaining insight into your behavior."

"Thanks, Amy," I said with a weak grin. I didn't buy most of what she said but I didn't want to rock the boat any further. So she patted me on the forehead and left the room.

I lay thinking about the recurring nightmares about Ariel. I knew in my heart something wasn't right. I resolved to do everything in my power to keep Ariel from riding a horse. But maybe the dreams were symbolic. I was flying high on Ariel's behalf and she was struggling with- what? Perhaps the death of her love for Teddy. Her dreams trampled. I was going round in circles until gradually I fell asleep.

I awoke to the call for meds. Amy and Angela, the day nurse, both asked me how I'd slept as my turn to get meds came. I told them that the Ativan helped. Then I realized I was still in my pyjamas. I said that I was going to get dressed now.

"That would be a good idea, Don," said a slightly amused, but at the same time sympathetic, Angela.

"I'll see you tomorrow, Don. Have a good day," said Amy.

"You mean there's no chance of me getting out today. Or Ariel?"

"You'll have to discuss that with Dr. Hilton. It's only an hour until your appointment with him. So, in the meantime, get dressed and wash up for breakfast." I knew that Amy had told me in a nice way that there wasn't a hope in hell for me to get out today. Then, I recalled that at least I would be here with Ariel. Provided she wasn't discharged, which I highly doubted since she'd been in seclusion several times. But you never know about hospitals.

I went for breakfast in the dayroom after dressing and grooming, and I saw Ariel eating breakfast with Jay and a female patient. I got my tray and I asked Ariel and Jay if I could join them. They said yes, and introduced me to Valery, Jay's new girlfriend. I said that maybe we could double date once we were out of here. They laughed.

"Dutch treat, as well," joked Jay.

We laughed again as I sat next to Ariel. I was almost crowding her efforts to eat her breakfast, I was so close to her.

But she smiled at me and ate her pancakes and sausages.

"I see Dr. Hilton today. Do you guys know what he's like?" I asked.

"He's okay," said Jay.

"I like him," added Valery. "He's helped me a lot. I was suicidal until he prescribed Zoloft for me."

"Oh, I've been on that," said Ariel. "But it didn't do much for me."

"I hear he likes to experiment with people's meds a lot," I continued.

"No, he's all right, Don. Don't believe most of the stuff you hear in here. Except from us four."

Again we laughed.

They finished their breakfasts before me, and Ariel told me that she was going to have a shower and that she'd see me later- after my appointment with Dr. Hilton.

"Take care, hon," I said, kissing Ariel quickly on the mouth.

"You, too," she answered, and departed from the dayroom. I finished my breakfast, put my tray away, and began to pace the halls in nervous anticipation of meeting the doctor.

"Don, you can come with me now," said Angela as I approached the nurses' office. "It's time to see Dr. Hilton."

We walked down the hall towards the TV room, and Angela knocked on a door just before there. We were told to come in. We entered the office.

"Hello, Don," said Dr. Hilton, holding out his hand. He was a big man with an imposing presence and a powerful handshake.

"Hello, Dr. Hilton," I replied.

"Please have a seat. You too, Angela." He motioned us into chairs. "So how are things going, Don?"

"Better. I'm not hearing voices and I'm not as mixed up."

"What were you mixed up about?" he asked very gently.

"I was mixed up about Ariel, I guess. She's also here and I'm in love with her."

"So, do you think the voices and being mixed up are connected with your feelings for her?"

"Yes, I do."

"And do you find that the medications have helped you deal with your symptoms of illness and your feelings towards her?"

"I guess so."

"Don, it is very important that you tell us how you feel, especially on the newer medications. Is the Olanzapine helping?"

"Well, now that you mention it, maybe Olanzapine has helped me. I feel like I'm ready to go home. Hopefully with Ariel."

"Don, how have you been relating to people other than Ariel?" asked Angela. I thought it was a loaded question.

"Not too bad. I made some friends."

"Do you keep to yourself a great deal, Don?" inquired Dr. Hilton.

"Sometimes."

"I get the feeling that you are sitting on top of many buried feelings."

"Aren't we all?" I was getting uneasy at this line of questioning.

"Don," interjected Angela, "it is important to gain insight into your feelings and illness. Many people with schizophrenia lack the growth potential that you have. You are on the 'high end,' which means your symptoms are more manageable. You will find that as you get in touch with your feelings and mature, you will start interacting with people again."

"Well put, Angela."

"Well, I'm not just another pretty face!" We all laughed, and I was glad that the tension had eased.

"Do you have any questions, Don?" asked Dr. Hilton.

"Yes. How long will I be here?"

"That depends on you. But I don't see it being too much longer. Remember, there are some very ill people on this ward, so try to control your impulses towards people socially." I knew he meant stop touching and kissing Ariel so much.

"So that means maybe I should be very cautious speaking with others."

"Yes. But getting back to your medications, I would like to keep you on Ativan- it helped you with your sleep after your bad dream last night. You are presently taking two milligrams a day, plus the

PRN which means you decide if you need extra. Or sometimes a nurse will ask you. The Luvox we'll leave for now at the same dosage. As for the Olanzapine, you are on ten milligrams, which is an average dose. Are you happy with that?"

"Yes. Overall, I feel pretty good."

"Very good, Don. Angela, do you have anything you'd like to add?"

"Yes. Don, have you had any side effects you've noticed from the new medications?"

"Good question, Angela," said Dr. Hilton.

"No. But if I do, I'll let you know."

"Very good, Don. Keep up the good work. We'll talk again soon," said Dr. Hilton, rising to shake my hand.

I followed Angela out of the office, and told her that I was going to my room to lie down. I realized I was tired from the meeting with the doctor, and I mentioned this to Angela. She nodded, saying she knew. I felt somewhat foolish after I laid down to rest, having told her something so obvious.

I thought of Ariel, and I began to fantasize about kissing her, feeling her breasts, making love to her. I fancied us being married and getting jobs and buying a house together to raise a family in. We would be as passionately in love ten years from now as we were today. I began to picture us horseback-riding with our children, but suddenly I was riding Pegasus into the red eye of sun, looking down on eagles and their aeries, while far below Ariel rode Teddy. I panicked and turned Pegasus back towards Ariel. Our children had disappeared, but I yelled "No! No! No!" as I saw Ariel fall from Teddy into a wheatfield. She rose foaming at the mouth, and then her knees buckled and she collapsed, her face turning into a skull-and-crossbones. I hollered "Ariel" at the top of my voice.

The next thing I knew Angela was waking me, saying I had had a bad dream again. She handed me some Ativan as I told her about my recurring nightmare. She said it was only a dream brought on by stress and that there was nothing to be overly concerned about. The Ativan should help, she added.

I rose from my bed, thanking Angela, and I said that I was going to have a coffee.

"It's lunch time in ten minutes, Don," Angela said softly, "but a group of us are going for coffee at the restaurant down the street this afternoon. Do you feel up to going?"

"Yes, I'd love to. Do you know if Ariel's going?"

"Yes, she is, but we're to stay in a group and socialize with everyone. You won't be alone with her."

"Oh, I wasn't thinking that. I'm just glad that she's coming with us."

"Okay, well maybe you should get washed up for lunch," Angela said, her eyes searching mine to see where I was. I agreed and did so; then I paced the halls looking for Ariel. Lunch would be brought in to the ward at any moment now. As I passed by the doctor's office I could hear Ariel's voice coming from the TV room. I went in and found Ariel alone, talking on the phone.

"I have to go now, Grandma, but I'll see you soon," she said very hurriedly, which sounded suspicious to me.

"You didn't have to hang up because of me, Ariel," I said as gently as possible.

"I know, but it's almost lunch time. Besides, I wanted to be with you, Don. I heard you shout my name a while ago. You sounded very frightened. Are you okay?"

"Oh, yeah, I'm all right. It was just a bad dream."

"Thanks a lot, Don. So dreams about me are bad!" She brushed past me before I could answer her. I threw my arms in the air in frustration. Then, Angela entered the TV room and told me lunch was ready. I told her about what had happened between me and Ariel, but she said not to worry, that it was just a misunderstanding.

"She'll be over it soon," said Angela, patting me on the shoulder as we left the TV room for the dayroom. I was feeling down as a flounder. I noticed Ariel was sitting with some older women, with her back to me, so I sat down beside Dale. He was very quiet again. I began to eat my lunch, although I didn't feel hungry. I turned to Dale while I glanced over at Ariel's gorgeous black flow of hair.

"Are you coming with us for coffee today, Dale?" I asked, hoping to pick up his mood.

"No."

I didn't question him any further after his curt response. I finished my lunch and glanced at Ariel, who was still talking to the ladies at her table. I wondered if she was talking about me. I put my empty tray back just as Angela came to me and told me to go get my meds. I had wanted to talk to Ariel, but I was certain Angela had intervened because she felt the time wasn't right for me to approach Ariel. I left the dayroom in a mood as down as a duck's feathers. My heart felt as heavy and blue as a blue whale, I thought to myself.

I was the first to finish my lunch, and then something strange came into my mind: I couldn't remember what I ate! As I got my meds, I told Angela, who had followed me, that I couldn't recall what I had had for lunch.

"You had a ham sandwich with chicken noodle soup. And a Canada Dry can of ginger ale. Don, you're stressed over Ariel. Don't worry so much. Maybe you should rest up before going for coffee at one."

I nodded, and turned around to see my friend Murray, from Solgate our boarding-home, coming down the hall.

"Hey, Don," he said, "how's it going?"

"Not too bad. I'm glad you came to visit. How are you?"

"Good. I just thought I'd say hi after going to the dentist's down the street."

"The dentist's? That can be almost as bad as being in here."

"I hear ya. But luckily I only had a cleaning."

"You know Ariel's in here, too? Well, of course you must. What a dumb question," I said, wanting to see his reaction.

"Yeah, I thought I'd say hi to her too. Are you still going out with her?"

"Why do you ask?" I said suspiciously.

"I need to tell you something about her. Can we go somewhere private?"

"How about my room?" I replied, feeling a surge of alarm and paranoia.

We entered my room and Murray sat in a chair; I sat on my bed facing him.

"What is it you wanted to tell me about Ariel?"

"It's about her ex-boyfriend, Stan. He came to the house looking for Ariel. He met Archie in the parking lot, and before the staff could talk to Stan, Archie said Ariel was in this psychiatric ward. But you know Archie, he would never try to fink or cause trouble. He's just not with it."

"I know Archie's not a bad guy. So when did this happen?"

"This morning. About ten. The staff can't do anything about it though, because Stan didn't do anything wrong. But I'd keep an eye on Ariel."

"I do all the time, anyhow," I said, frowning.

"Okay. I'm sorry to be the bringer of bad news but I wanted you to know. Because I know how much you care for Ariel."

"Thanks, Murr."

"So do you know when you're getting out yet?"

I asked him to repeat the question because I was becoming distraught over Ariel. He asked again.

"Oh... um...no. Not yet. What do you think this Stan guy will do if he meets Ariel?"

"I don't know. But I've heard he's no good for her."

"Thanks, Murr."

We talked about the staff and residents at Solgate for awhile, and then Murray said he had to leave but before he did, he wanted to say hi to Ariel. I told him Ariel wasn't speaking to me just now, but she'd probably come around in a little while. We were about to leave my room, when Angela came in and announced to me that the ward's coffee outing would be in ten minutes. I introduced her to Murray. They shook hands and Angela told me to dress warm. The three of us left my room.

We saw Ariel coming out of the smoking room down the hall, and she said loudly and enthusiastically "Hi, Murray! It's great to see you! How've you been?"

"Hi, Ariel. I'm fine. And yourself?"

She walked directly towards Murray and, ignoring me, gave him a big hug, while kissing him on the neck. Angela spoke to Ariel, telling her to get a warm coat or jacket on for the coffee outing. Murray looked at me as they disengaged themselves, and said he had to be going. He wished Ariel and I all the best.

Ariel turned away and went towards her room. I was going to follow her but Angela told me to get ready for the outing. I put on my blue jacket, feeling apprehensive and almost sick to my stomach.

## ❧ Chapter 12 ☙

While waiting for the others, I asked Angela who all would be going on the coffee outing.

"You, me, Ariel, Jay, Valery, and a new nurse named Julia. We won't be gone very long– the restaurant is only a block away."

The rest of the group was ready a minute later and we collected by the nurses' station. I noticed Ariel was a vision of blue: jeans, jean-jacket, azure sweater, and blue sneakers. She had her hair down, and wore more make-up than I'd ever seen her wear. I tried to catch her eye, but she wouldn't look at me. I was devastated, though determined to be with her.

As we left the ward, Angela and Julia said to stay together at all times. I felt like I was in kindergarten as I'm sure the others did, too. Julia and Ariel walked in front of Angela and me, while Jay and Valery brought up the behind. I was desperate to talk to Ariel, so I began to walk faster down the white halls, but Angela grabbed my sleeve and said not to interrupt Ariel and Julia, that they were getting to know each other. I felt angry as a disturbed bear. So, we went in three pairs down the steps instead of the elevator. Angela thought we could use the exercise, and she was right. It felt good to be off the ward; I only hoped Ariel would come around from her snit and talk to me.

We finished the four flights of stairs, walked past the gift shop, then the reception area, and finally we were out in the cool, autumn air. I almost forgot about Ariel as I looked around at the people walking towards the hospital. I knew we looked conspicuous, but I was grateful we could look at trees, birds, and flowers as we walked down the sidewalk.

"Are you feeling okay, Don?" asked Angela.

"Yes. I was just enjoying the view. You know, Ariel's butt." Angela and I laughed.

"Are you—I've been meaning to ask—a Psychiatric Nurse or a Registered Nurse?" I asked Angela.

"I'm a Registered Nurse. But I'm planning on someday going to med school to be a doctor like my father was. He retired two years ago, and said he'd back me all the way if I wanted to be a doctor. He was educated at Harvard, and has a lot of influence. He still lectures at universities all over North America."

"My doctor lectures, too," I said.

"Really?" she asked, surprised.

"Yeah, he lectures me." We laughed so hard, Ariel and Julia turned to find out what we were joking about. I smiled at Ariel, but she haughtily turned away. I felt a tightness in my chest when I began to believe that Ariel thought that I was talking and joking about her. I was going to mention this fear to Angela but we had reached the restaurant, and we went inside in a close group.

It was a fast food restaurant so we wouldn't have to wait long for our drinks. Angela took our orders after we were seated in a large booth. Ariel was sitting across from me, looking uncharacteristically antsy and nervous. She looked at her watch, as Angela went with Jay to get our drinks. I had ordered a coke, the same as Ariel had.

"Can I go to the washroom, Julia?" asked Ariel, ignoring me.

"I guess so. But hurry it up if you can."

Ariel got up and went past the counter towards the washrooms, then suddenly she ran out of the restaurant doors and into the parking lot. Within seconds, through the glass windows we could see a blue pick-up truck pull up with two men in it; Ariel jumped in and was gone with them before Angela or Julia could stop her.

Angela pulled out a cell phone and phoned the police, giving descriptions of Ariel and the truck. I wondered why Ariel would do such a thing; then, I remembered the suspicious phone call earlier today. So, she planned to leave me and– could that have been Stan driving the truck? I interjected in my thought processes. I felt like a beaten dog.

Julia helped Jay bring the coffees and cokes to our table, and Angela phoned the psychiatric ward. When she got off the phone, she asked if everyone was all right. Jay said it wasn't the first time he'd seen a mental patient run away– and it probably wouldn't be the last. I noticed I was shaking as I drank my coke. Apparently Angela noticed too, and asked how I was doing. I said that I was very worried about Ariel. She said we all were, and that Ariel would be okay.

We finished our drinks as the police arrived. They took down the necessary information about Ariel and left. The walk back to the hospital was very quiet and tense. I was holding in my tears as we reached the psychiatric ward. I guessed that I hadn't flipped out because of the new meds, especially since I was convinced that Ariel no longer loved me. I mentioned these things to Angela, and she agreed. Then she told me to try to relax with a cup of tea.

I walked down the halls towards the dayroom. Jay was pouring coffee for himself and Valery. I asked him if he had seen Stan in the truck that Ariel got into, but he said he hadn't seen the men's faces. He said to try not to worry, and he and Valery excused themselves because they were going for a smoke. They carried their coffees into the smoking room just as Nancy came into the dayroom.

"Why Luke, you haven't destroyed the Deathstar yet," she said.

"I'm going to lie down, Nancy. See ya," I said, and left the dayroom rather hastily.

"You must destroy the Deathstar before it destroys you!" she shouted at me.

"Nancy, stop bothering people," said Angela.

I told Angela I was going to rest. I went and slithered onto my bed, exhausted and stressed with worry. I began to dream that I was riding Pegasus high above the eagles and their aeries when I noticed Ariel riding Teddy far below in a wheatfield near the foam of the ocean tide. Suddenly, she was tossed and landed on her back. I shouted "No!" and drove Pegasus all the way down to her side. When I saw her face turn into a skull-and-croossbones, I panicked and screamed Ariel's name.

I awoke to see Dr. Hilton, Angela, Julia, and other staff in my room along with two police officers. Dr. Hilton asked me if I knew where Ariel had gone. I was groggy, but shook my head no. He asked me if I'd given her any money or bank card. I said no. Then I asked what the hell all the questions were for. Dr. Hilton said very gently that Ariel had used my bank card to get money for drugs. She had overdosed with Stan on heroin, or "horse" as they called it. They had both passed away in a downtown hotel room this afternoon.

"We're sorry, Don. We know how much you loved Ariel," said Angela.

"We have Stan's friend in custody, and he confessed that Ariel told him that she had stolen your bank card the day you were in the shower with her. And she had gotten your personal code in the pub. She was an alcoholic and drug user, Don," said a tall RCMP officer.

"You just couldn't see it," said Angela.

"And now I can' t see her!" I cried out.

"Get some rest, Don. Or if you need to talk, don't hesitate to approach us."

They left the room, as I wept bitterly with my face buried in my pillow.

"Ariel, I'll always love you," I said, my voice muffled.

Printed in the United Kingdom
by Lightning Source UK Ltd.
111236UKS00001B/131